TERROR STALKS
THE BORDER

TERROR STALKS THE BORDER

A WESTERN DUO

LESLIE SCOTT

Five Star • Waterville, Maine

Five Star First Edition Western Series.

Published in 2002 in conjunction with Golden West Literary Agency.

Cover design by Thorndike Press Staff.

Set in 11 pt. Plantin by Minnie B. Raven.

Printed in the United States on permanent paper.

Library of Congress Cataloging-in-Publication Data

Scott, Leslie, 1893–1975.
    [Knight of the silver star]
    Terror stalks the border : a western duo /
by Leslie Scott.
        p. cm.—(Five Star first edition western series)
    ISBN 0-7862-3537-3 (hc : alk. paper)
    Contents: Knight of the silver star—Terror stalks the border.
    1. Western stories. I. Scott, Leslie, 1893–1975.
Terror stalks the border. II. Title. III. Series.
PS3537.C9265 K58 2002
  813'.52—dc21   2002276823

TABLE OF CONTENTS

FOREWORD
BY
ALBERT TONIK

Alexander Leslie Scott was born on January 15, 1893 in Lewisburg, West Virginia. Whether it has any bearing on his life or not, it is claimed that the winter at the beginning of 1893 was one of the toughest West Virginia has ever experienced. His father was a ninth generation Virginian descended from Samuel Scott. His mother had rifle-toting uncles in West Virginia named Hatfield. To his friends and relatives he was Leslie. His family called him Les. He died in 1974, when he was eighty-one. He had been sick for a few years before that. However, he wrote stories until almost the end. When he published a story, sometimes he would use a pseudonym. When he used his own name, he shortened it to A. Leslie.

His mother was Justina Blazer and came from the Hatfield family. The feud between the Hatfields and the McCoys started in 1878 and lasted until 1889. The Hatfields lived in West Virginia just across the border from Kentucky. The McCoys lived across the river in Kentucky. The leader of the Hatfield clan was Devil Anse Hatfield, and that of the McCoy clan was Old Ranel McCoy.

Old Ranel had Floyd Hatfield arrested for stealing one of his pigs. The jury acquitted Floyd. Several McCoys fought with and killed a Hatfield. They pleaded self-defense and were acquitted. Then three McCoys seriously wounded Ellison Hatfield. The three were arrested. However, on the

7

way to jail, Devil Anse Hatfield kidnapped them. When Ellison Hatfield died, the three McCoy brothers were executed by the Hatfields. Kentucky issued rewards for the capture of the Hatfields, and this led to a number of battles against the Hatfields. At one point there was a shoot-out at the post office. In retaliation, some Hatfields attacked the McCoy home and burned it, killing two children. Eight Hatfields got life sentences. That ended the hostilities. After twelve years and twelve deaths, the feud was over.

As a boy Leslie spent some time climbing around cliffs and crawling through caves in West Virginia. In 1904 he started reading *The Argosy,* one of the popular pulp magazines with stories from all genres. Afterward, he would read it whenever he could find a copy.

When he was fourteen, his father arranged a summer job on a cattle boat that sailed from the United States to England. In London, he jumped ship and continued around the world. He sent his parents a postcard from Cairo. He continued to India, and then to Singapore. He worked on a pearling schooner in the South Seas and fought his way up to third mate.

For education, Leslie attended Greenbrier Military Academy, the University of West Virginia, and the graduate school at the University of Virginia. He studied mining and civil engineering in college and graduate school. Many of his stories revolve around the proper way to discover, or mine, oil, gold, silver, copper, mercury, or radium.

While at school his summer vacations were filled with excitement and adventures. He learned the cattle business while working on his uncle's ranch in Texas. He learned about firearms while riding with Pancho Villa, and he may have handled a machine gun. Leslie's excursion into Mexico with the forces of Pancho Villa probably occurred

8

in 1914. Villa was born Doroteo Arango in 1877 in Mexico. As a youth he became a bandit and changed his name to Francisco "Pancho" Villa. He organized a ring of cattle rustlers that caused a price to be placed on his head. He also lived in a time of violent political upheavals. From 1910 to 1913 there were three revolts that ousted the head of a Mexican government and replaced him with another. Pancho Villa gathered an army and aided the first of these revolutions. He was captured, but managed to escape to the United States. There he organized another army and helped the third revolution. In this one he was able to march into Mexico City before being routed. Probably Leslie was involved in this last revolt.

In the middle of 1914, the Great War began. Leslie signed up with the French Foreign Legion. He spent four years fighting in the trenches. He became an officer. When seventy senior officers were killed in one battle, Leslie was elevated to the battlefield rank of major. At the end of the war, he was brevetted a captain.

When Leslie returned to civilian life after the end of the war, he got a job on the Chesapeake & Ohio Railroad, shoveling coal. The route ran near New River and along the mountain roads of West Virginia and Ohio. Later he wrote some stories for the pulp magazine, *Railroad Stories*. In that magazine, it was stated that A. Leslie was an ex-brakeman, yet he was a member of The Brotherhood of Locomotive Firemen. Leslie claimed he was a fireman, a conductor, and a brakeman at different times. He called certainly upon this background when he wrote stories about railroading, namely, how a locomotive works, how tracks are laid, how grades are made, how tunnels are dug, how bridges are built.

When Leslie left the railroad, he fell back upon his college training and went West to work in mining engineering and bridge building. Again these themes would be used in many of his later stories concerned with the building of tunnels or bridges, especially how explosives are used in mines and tunnels; how bridges are built across rivers or streams to withstand the unusual forces of a torrent of water caused by a cloud burst; how to build a wire conveyer system to bring buckets of ore down the side of a mountain.

During this period, in the mid 1920s, he began to be published. At first he composed poems. He sold these to newspapers and magazines. In those days, newspaper and magazines bought poetry to fill up space. The first poem that appeared in a pulp magazine was "The Moon Dance" in the May 1926 issue of *Weird Tales*. The magazine was subtitled "the unique magazine" because its stories emphasized the supernatural. The first line of Leslie's poem is:

***Throbbing drums, a cold, dead moon.* . . .**

For the next two years, poems like this by Leslie Scott appeared in *Weird Tales* about every other month. Then they fell off to one or two a year until 1935. However, by 1930 he was also selling about five stories a year to various pulp magazines and by 1935 that figure had grown to ten stories a year.

About 1930, Leslie Scott gave up his engineering career in the West altogether, moved to New York, and concentrated on his writing career. When President Franklin D. Roosevelt entered office in 1932, he started several projects to try to move people into paying jobs to combat the Great Depression. One of his efforts was the Work Projects Administration, and a WPA program consisted of setting up free classes in New York City to teach people new trades. In

1934, Lily Kay, who was born in 1913, signed up for a course in art. She arrived late at the school to attend the first session. She asked an attendant where the classroom was. He pointed to a door. Hoping not to be noticed or to disturb the class already in session, she entered quietly and took a seat, but a mistake had been made. This was a class on how to write, not on how to draw. She was too embarrassed to leave. She stayed. It was interesting. She came back for the rest of the lectures. One of the guest lecturers was Alexander Leslie Scott. After several sessions he asked her out to dinner. This led eventually to their marriage on August 29, 1937, a marriage that lasted thirty-seven years. Lily K. Scott became the author of love stories and true confessions. Their union begat a son, Justin, born on July 20, 1944, and a daughter, Alison, born on July 18, 1946. Both children also became authors.

Alexander Leslie Scott fulfilled a boyhood dream when he began publishing his fiction in *Argosy*. In 1935 he began contributing detective stories to *The Phantom Detective* and *G-Men Detective*, adventure stories to *Thrilling Adventures*, and had Western stories published in *All Western*, *Thrilling Ranch Stories*, and *Thrilling Western*. *All Western* was a Dell publication, while all the others were published by Standard Magazines, some under subsidiary names such as Better Publications, Phantom Detective, Inc., Rugby House, and Metropolitan Magazines. Standard Magazines was known as the Thrilling Group because most of the titles of their magazines were *Thrilling* something or other.

All the pulps published by Standard Magazines were under the editorial directorship of Leo Margulies, known as "The Little Giant of the Pulps." He was short, not over five feet five inches, very dynamic, and had control at one time of about twenty-five magazines. He had many assistant edi-

11

tors who read the manuscripts and sent their comments to Margulies, who would then decide to buy or reject. The desk in his office was on a raised platform so that he could look down on his assistants or visitors. He established a cadre of writers who could sell their stories directly to Standard Magazines without having to go through a literary agency. Once a writer became a member of this cadre, Margulies would buy practically every story written by that writer, very few ever being rejected. In an emergency, when one of the cadre needed money, Margulies would issue a voucher for the paymaster to pay the writer an advance on a promised story. When the story was received and approved, Margulies would pay the remainder of the money due the author.

Leslie Scott became a member of Leo Margulies's cadre. In a conversation between the two, Margulies told Leslie that to insure a steady income he would have to begin writing a series of stories about the same character and have them published in a monthly magazine. At the time the news media was carrying stories about the centenary of the birth of the Texas Rangers. Margulies thought it would be a good idea to start a magazine featuring stories about the Texas Rangers.

Leslie was asked to write the feature story for the new *Texas Rangers*, that would be launched with the October 1936 issue. Leslie, who was beginning to feel comfortable writing Westerns, agreed. He invented a Texas Ranger named James Hatfield. The Hatfield name was in honor of his mother's relatives. In these stories, Hatfield always said: "First name sorta got whittled down to Jim." Actually Leslie Scott had previously used the Hatfield name for Arizona Ranger Rance Hatfield, the hero of "The Arizona Ranger" in *Thrilling Western* (6/35), and in "Justice on the

Range" in *Thrilling Western* (1/36). When Leslie's Jim Hatfield made his debut in *Texas Rangers*, the author's name was given as Jackson Cole, a house name at Standard Magazines. A publisher would use a house name to hide the identity of the real author and thus have the ability to publish future stories about the same character by different authors without the public being aware of any change in authorship. Obvious reasons for switching actual authors in a series are that the first author might die, or get tired of writing about the same character, or not produce stories fast enough, or want too much money.

The origin of the Jackson Cole name has a complex history. A number of reference books say that it was the pen name for Oscar Shisgall (2/23/01–5/20/84). In a letter, dated April 6, 1982, Oscar Shisgall explained that, when he began to write Westerns, an editor suggested that Oscar Shisgall was not an appropriate name for a Western author, so he adopted the name Jackson Cole. It has been further suggested that Jackson Cole may be a variation of Jackson Hole, Wyoming. However, when Oscar Shisgall gave up writing Westerns, Leo Margulies asked if he could keep the name as a house name at Standard Magazines. Shisgall said he had no more use for the Jackson Cole name and Margulies could use it any way he desired. This release of the Jackson Cole name occurred before *Texas Rangers* started. Oscar Shisgall never had anything to do with the Jim Hatfield stories.

Checking Oscar Shisgall's bibliography in the pulps and Jackson Cole's bibliography shows something of interest. Shisgall began writing detective stories for the pulps in 1922. He wrote some Westerns from 1933 to 1938. One interesting fact was that the latter date was long after Standard Magazines began using the name, Jackson Cole, as the author of the Jim Hatfield stories. Another curious fact is that all of Oscar Shisgall's pulp Westerns were published under his own name, and not under the Jackson Cole name. However, Oscar Shisgall did have about ten of his Western pulp novels published in hard cover books. These book editions all bore the name Jackson Cole. So it would appear that the editor, who first suggested the change of name, worked for Shisgall's book publisher. These books were published from 1933 to 1937. The later date was after the first Jim Hatfield story had already appeared on the newsstands.

Another interesting question is when did the Jackson Cole name first begin to appear in pulp magazines? Leo Margulies began using this name as the author of adventure tales as early as 1933. This was approximately at the same time that Oscar Shisgall was using the name for some of his hard cover books. Were these pulp stories written by Oscar Shisgall? Had Oscar Shisgall forgotten that he had given Leo Margulies permission to use the Jackson Cole name for pulp stories while he was still using it for books he had written? These questions are as yet without answers.

When Leslie Scott began writing the Jim Hatfield stories for *Texas Rangers*, he had been writing stories with lengths varying between 2,000 and 20,000 words. Most of his stories had been running about 10,000 words. All of a sudden he was being asked to write stories of 40,000 words. He had to strain to reach that length and often resorted to adding incident after incident without really advancing the story. As a result, the early Jim Hatfield stories seem rather choppy.

The first three issues of *Texas Rangers* were bi-monthly. Leslie was able to supply Jim Hatfield stories at that rate. When the magazine went monthly, Leslie could no longer make the deadlines. Leo Margulies brought in other writers to fill the gap. For the ninth issue, August 1937, Tom Curry filled in for Leslie, and from then on Tom Curry and Leslie Scott alternated on almost a regular basis until the November 1951 issue. In these years each author wrote about fifty-five Jim Hatfield stories apiece.

Leslie's ability to write these longer stories improved with each story. By the time of the tenth Jim Hatfield story (Scott's seventh), Leslie was able to write a consistent tale. It flowed from beginning to end. This story, "Terror Stalks the Border," appeared in the September 1937 issue of *Texas Rangers* and is the one included in this volume.

Jim Hatfield is an unusual character. Mentally he is a genius. He can reach instantaneous decisions and act on them. He has the mind of a great detective. He can analyze situations and small clues and decide who is the guilty party. He believes that everyone could be a good citizen of Texas and deserves his protection, whether that person is a wealthy ranch owner, a working cowboy, a sheepherder, a nester, an Indian, or a Mexican *peón*. This is consistent with Leslie Scott himself who believed in the equality of all men, regardless of their race, color, or religion.

Physically Jim Hatfield is well over six feet tall. He has great strength. He can outfight and outwrestle almost everyone he meets. He is not handsome, but he has rugged good looks. His eyes are green-gray. Most of the time his eyes are a merry green, but when he is angry, his eyes become "a shade of snow-dusted ice on a bitter winter morning." He carries two guns at his waist, and he can outdraw and outshoot, with either hand, practically everyone he meets.

Incidentally, Leslie Scott could almost be describing himself when he described Jim Hatfield. Leslie was tall (over six feet) and brawny. He had trained as a boxer at school. He could beat almost anyone in arm wrestling (this was true even when he was almost sixty years old).

Most of the Jim Hatfield stories seem to be set in the 1890s with railroads being built and barbed-wire fences being erected. There are deprecations that the local law could not handle, rustling, murders, disappearances, wire cutting, a Ranger being killed, range wars. A letter goes to the Texas Rangers asking for a troop to be sent. A troop cannot be spared. Captain Bill McDowell, who supposedly "would charge hell with a bucket of water," sends Jim Hatfield without notifying anyone he is coming. Jim arrives at the scene, dressed as an ordinary cowhand with his badge hidden, riding his magnificent stallion, Goldy. Jim gets hired as a cowboy, a foreman, or a shotgun guard on a stage. There is always a greedy, hidden mastermind behind all the deprivations. Jim gathers clues as he fights against the invisible outlaws. At the end, he puts on his badge and has a showdown with the real villain. All the citizens recognize this Texas Ranger and remark with awe that only one Ranger was needed to handle the situation. There is a resemblance to "The Lone Ranger" on radio. Jim is known as the Lone Wolf. He rides a horse called Goldy, instead of Silver.

Leslie Scott loved to use a certain number of pet phrases. In talking about a gambling hall, he would always call it a gambling hell. Whenever Jim Hatfield ate at a restaurant, he usually ordered hog's hip and cackle berries. The cook always understood that he wanted one of America's favorite breakfast dishes. Whenever a scene had no light, it was always black dark. Whenever violent action occurs, one of the characters usually says: "You shore raised hell and shoved a chunk under a corner." When a gambler deals cards, they slither across the cloth.

Things went well with Leslie for a while. He was producing a Jim Hatfield story every two months and getting paid $400 for each one. Then in 1938 *Texas Rangers* magazine returned to being a bi-monthly. Since Tom Curry was also producing Jim Hatfield stories, Scott's income took a nose dive, and he had a wife to support. By the end of 1939, he knew he had to do something else. He began a second series of stories about a Texas Ranger called Walt Slade. These were published in *Thrilling Western*, also a bi-monthly pulp magazine. The Walt Slade stories were shorter, being only about 15,000 words, and for each he was paid $150. He was able to produce six of these stories a year. For these stories he used the name Bradford Scott.

Walt Slade was Jim Hatfield with a different name. His horse, instead of being tawny, is black and is called Shadow. Slade's nickname is El Halcón, The Hawk. Slade is an undercover operative for Captain McNelty. At the end of each story, he kills the arch villain and so acquires the reputation of being an outlaw. The real distinguishing feature about Walt Slade is that he carries a guitar with him and sings with a marvelous voice.

Leslie Scott had almost seventy Walt Slade stories published in *Thrilling Western*, beginning in March, 1940 with "Knight of the Silver Star" and ending in March, 1951 with "Trail from Yesterday." The first Walt Slade story is included here.

Leslie Scott's most interesting period is during the 1940s. Here his work is strong and fresh. After that, he seemed to run out completely of fresh ideas and some of the scenes in later stories would repeat scenes from earlier works. Nevertheless, his stories continued to be published during the 1950s and 1960s as original paperback books and sold well. During the last twenty years of his life, he wrote and sold between eight to twelve paperback novels a year, an amazing feat when you consider that he was in his sixties and seventies.

From 1940 to 1951 he was selling between ten and fifteen Western stories a year to the pulp magazines. Between 1936 and 1946, he took about fifteen of his Jim Hatfield stories, revised and enlarged them, and sold them to hard cover book publishers under the name Jackson Cole. These expansions often consisted of taking a short story and re-writing it to fit into the middle of a Jim Hatfield adventure. Ned Pines, the president of Standard Magazines, objected to Leslie using the Jackson Cole name and to re-selling stories to which Pines had bought all rights. Leslie continued to do this, despite the objections, conceding only changing the hero's name from Jim Hatfield and his horse's name and eventually changing his byline to Bradford Scott, or A. Leslie, and finally writing everything as Leslie Scott. He would intersperse these expanded books with original novels.

It was when the pulp magazines died that Leslie switched to writing paperback novels. In 1956 he wrote a half dozen Jim Hatfield stories as Jackson Cole. Again Ned Pines objected. Leslie switched to Walt Slade stories by Bradford Scott. During the next seventeen years he wrote over one hundred Walt Slade novels that had composite sales of eight million copies.

What were Leslie Scott's writing habits? He would wake after noon. He would spend the afternoons playing with his children or visiting neighbors. He was active in Boy Scouts and coached in Little League. After the children were put to bed, he would set his typewriter on the kitchen table and write all night. Only after the children were grown, did he change his schedule to writing during the day.

Because he had moved his family outside New York City, once a week Leslie would take the train into the city to visit with his editors. Walking to the train station, he passed by the houses of many neighbors. All the dogs in the neighborhood knew him. They would come over for a pet and follow him to the train station. Quite frequently the train would have to stop just outside of the village where Leslie lived so the conductor could chase these dogs off the train. Animals, unlike human beings, cannot be deceived about a person's character.

KNIGHT OF THE SILVER STAR

I

"ON WINGS OF SONG"

Moonlight, like silver rain, streamed through the thin gauze of cloud that veiled the sultry Texas sky. Under its soft touch, the gaunt lines of spire and crag were blurred and mellowed, and the weirdly brandished arms of giant cacti cast grotesque shadows across the desert sands.

Through the thin flood of moonlight rode a man. He was nearly six feet tall, broad of shoulder, lean of waist. His face was deeply bronzed, high of cheek bone, high-bridged as to nose. The hair revealed by a pushed-back, broad-brimmed hat was thick and black. The mouth below the hooked nose was rather wide, grin-quirked at the corners. Beneath level black brows, laughing gray eyes looked out upon the world, and found it good. They were unusual, those merry eyes, for they had a habit of changing color slightly at times—and then there was but little of laughter in their depths.

"Billy the Kid had eyes like them," a tough old-timer who had looked into those eyes at a "wrong" time once said. "Uhn-huh, and Doc Holliday, and Buckskin Frank Leslie. Them damn' outlaw killers always seemed to have eyes what would grin at you one minute and look sudden death and destruction at you back of a gun sight the next!"

It almost seemed that the man drifted through the moonlight on invisible wings, rather than rode. The tall horse clamped between his muscular thighs was black as the night itself. Only the shimmer of moonlight, reflected by its satiny coat, told that it was there at all. The dainty hoofs made no sound in the sand, and the horse moved with a lithe grace that was muscular perfection.

The rider was booted and spurred. Shotgun chaps encased his overalled legs. He wore a faded blue shirt, and about his throat was looped, cowboy-style, a vivid handkerchief. Heavy double cartridge belts encircled the lean waist, and the black butts of long-barreled Colts showed above the carefully worked and oiled cut-out holsters. Across the saddle horn rested a small guitar, and the rider's supple fingers breathed across the strings as he sang a love song of old Spain.

In the Mexican quarter of the border town of Cholla, the *peónes* lifted their heads, and tired eyes brightened as the rich voice came borne to them on the wings of the wind.

"El Halcón. The Hawk," they murmured.

"*Ai,*" said a graybeard. "The Hawk. He rides again. And he sings. *Ai,* when he sings, some evil one soon will weep."

But the tall rider did not pause in the Mexican quarter, although hands were waved in greeting and soft-voiced invitations sounded as he passed by the humble dwellings. He had looped the guitar over his shoulder by a silken cord, and he waved a sinewy hand in reply, his teeth flashing startlingly white in his bronzed face.

It was contagious, that white grin, and the *peónes* smiled and laughed, and somehow the squalid quarter seemed brighter for his passing.

Only once did he pull the big horse to a halt. It was when a little girl with great liquid black eyes toddled out into the road. He leaned over, swept the crowing baby high into the air in the crook of one sinewy arm, and ruffled her black curls tenderly with his free hand.

Gently he set her down again in the moon-streaked dust, and she pattered back to her beaming mother, prattling delightedly and holding up a souvenir of her brief visit with El Halcón—a shiny .45 cartridge.

As is often the custom of men who ride much alone, the man talked to his horse.

"Reckon the first thing in order, Shadow, is to find some place where you can bed down and put on the nosebag. I can stand to surround a sizable helpin' or two of chuck myself, and I figger you must be gettin' kinda lank, too, you dad-blamed old grass burner!"

Shadow, the big horse, snorted general agreement and pricked his ears.

The rider tickled his sensitive ribs with his spurs, and Shadow squealed his anger and reached for a leg with gleaming teeth. The man the Mexicans had called El Halcón slapped the gelding's glossy neck affectionately with his wide hat, and they ambled on in mutual good humor.

"This appears to be quite a *pueblo*," The Hawk went on as lights began to appear with greater frequency and a babble of sound pierced through the monotonous drumming beat that continuously trembled the air.

The pounding rumble, The Hawk knew, was the never-ceasing dance of the giant stamps pulverizing the gold ore taken from the mines in the gaunt Cholla Hills, at whose base the town was built, just as he knew that the lively thumping sound, from the garishly glittering street he was approaching, was made by the muddy boots of the men who worked the mines.

"But those heels that are clickin' on the floor like a lady cayuse's hoofs on a frozen trail ain't got no mud on 'em," he told the black horse.

Shadow's answering snort seemed to indicate scant approval of the girls whose short skirts were swaying alongside the clumping boots of the miners. But his tall rider chuckled, and in the merry eyes was a light of anticipation.

"Oh, dance-hall gals ain't so bad, some of 'em," he disagreed. "Particularly after you've looked at 'em a few times through the bottom of a glass. Funny, how all *señoritas* seem to sorta look beautiful through the bottom of a glass. Oh, well, if that's the way you feel about it, I won't argue with you no more."

Other clicking sounds became apparent as they drew abreast of the lighted windows. There was the musical *clink* of bottlenecks against the rims of glasses, the sprightly *patter* of dice across a green cloth, the soft *slither* of cards, the merry chatter of roulette wheels.

Song, or what passed for it, bellowed forth to make the night something to forget. The soft *thrum* of guitars, the *whine* of fiddles, and the *pinging* of banjos provided cheerful melody for the dancers, and the *thumping* of hard fists on the mahogany furnished even more cheerful music for the saloonkeepers.

"Yeah, she's quite a town," The Hawk repeated, a speculative gleam in his gray eyes as the black horse *click-clacked* past a solidly constructed building with the word **BANK** legending the windows. "Money here, feller, plenty of it. Them stamp mills aren't poundin' just to make a noise, and all these drink jugglers aren't in business for their health. Gold comin' outta them hills up there, and lots of it circulatin' 'round. Yeah, I got a plumb notion you and me have come to the right place to do a little business for ourselves."

Glancing down a quieter side street, he turned the black's head. A few moments later they pulled up in front of a small livery stable. The Hawk shouted, and the sliding door creaked on its rollers.

The owner of the stable was tall, wide, and thick, with twinkling little brown eyes set in rolls of fat. His face was rubicund, his mouth a pursed button, and there were chuckle quirks at the corners, grin wrinkles around the eyes.

"OK," he squeaked in a voice like a pack rat with its tail in a crack.

The Hawk sent Shadow through the doorway, and the fat man had him in a stall and the hull off almost before the rider had swung leg to ground.

"The sort it's worth gettin' hanged for to steal," piped the fat man, admiring the black's beautiful lines.

The Hawk grinned, after he had unscrambled the sentence.

"Reckon you aren't insinuating anythin' personal," he replied, "but I agree with the general sentiments."

"Name's Oakes," remarked the fat man in conversational tones, "ordinarily and mostly known as Sliver."

The other glanced at him keenly, and the momentary hesitancy before he spoke was not lost on Sliver Oakes. "Slade is the handle I hang on when I sign the payroll," he vouchsafed at length. "The preacher said . . . Walter . . . when he slung water in my face. But that's sorta got whittled down to Walt in the twenty-five years what's loafed along since then."

Sliver Oakes nodded, still busy caring for the black horse. Walt Slade studied him, and nodded. "Don't reckon I need to be givin' any instructions," he commented. "You appear to know your business pretty well."

"I do," the other replied succinctly. "Twenty years cowpokin' 'fore I got too fat. Been hangin' out in this she-bang for another five. Reckon you know somethin' about the cow business, too. Nice rig you're usin'."

The Hawk nodded easily. "Yeah, I threw a rope or two in my time," he admitted. He did not miss Sliver Oakes's glance at his slim hands, and spread them wide, palms up. "Nope, I haven't thrown one in quite a spell, though," he said quietly.

Oakes's fat face flushed. "Wasn't meanin' nothin' personal," he squeaked. "You know an old-timer in the cow business sorta gets so he notices things. You weren't slow at catchin' onto how my glims was pointed yourself."

Walt Slade nodded again. "Reckon you know somethin' about itchy feet," he pointed out. "When a feller gets to trailin' his rope from one place to another, he don't do over much work for so long as his *dinero* holds out. I'm getting sorta low now, that's why I'm figgerin' on glommin' onto somethin' what'll divvy a few *pesos*."

"Reckon that's so," agreed Sliver, busying himself with bedding down Shadow. "Only, feller, you didn't get them calluses on your thumb and first finger from settin' on your hands," he muttered under his breath. "Mebbe you ain't done no cow chambermaidin' for a spell, but you shore been busy practicin' a fast draw!"

Walt Slade was rolling a cigarette with the slim fingers of his left hand. "Any place hereabouts where a feller can get a room?" he asked.

Sliver Oakes favored him with another shrewd glance. "I got one topside the stable," he said. "Two up there. I use one and rent t'other."

"Fine!" said Slade. "I'll take it."

"OK," agreed Oakes, "and you don't hafta."

"Don't have to what?"

"Don't hafta pay in advance. Mostly I makes young range-ridin' hellions of your sort plank the *pesos* down first before they get the room."

"Folks sort of honest hereabouts?"

"Nope, not that. Reckon they're about as fair to middlin' honest as in any other district, but this is a sorta unhealthy locality, particularly for a young feller with itchy trigger fingers who is lookin' for excitement. But, if somethin' breaks, I figger you'll look at the right end of your guns before you look into the wrong end of t'other feller's."

Walt Slade chuckled, but there was a peculiar light in his gray eyes. He unlooped the guitar from over his shoulder. "Put the music box in my room, will you, feller?" he said. "I figger on amblin' out and surrounding a helpin' of chuck before I pound my ear."

"If you like music," remarked Sliver, slipping the guitar into its waterproof case, "mosey over to Carry Farr's Brandin' Pen Saloon. They got a good Mex orchestra there, and some fellers what can sing. Good chuck, too, but a sorta salty crowd hangs out there. Turn left when you hit the main street, and it's jest a coupla leg shakes."

"Carry Farr? That's a funny-sounding handle," remarked Slade, as he headed for the door.

"Uhn-huh. Dot 'n' Carry is what the boys call him, but that was sorta of a mouthful for tired gents to spout, so folks mostly compromise on callin' him Carry."

II

"SONG OF THE GUN"

Slade had no difficulty locating the Branding Pen Saloon. He pushed through the swinging doors, still wondering about the proprietor's unusual name.

It was a big place, fairly well-lighted and well-crowded. An orchestra of guitars and muted violins was making music for the dancers that were gathered on the open space to one side of the poker tables and the roulette wheels. There was a lunch counter, tables along one wall for the accommodation of diners, and a bar that stretched the full length of the opposite wall.

Several perspiring drink jugglers were pouring whisky as fast as they could knock the necks from bottles. Gold was *clinking* on the mahogany, and more gold gleamed dully on the green cloth of the tables. The dance floor was busy, and the girls, mostly Mexicans, were good-looking and young.

Slade eyed them appreciatively, and at the same time his gaze did not fail to note the swift, appraising glances cast in his direction from various sources as he entered the saloon.

Gents here aren't missing any bets, he mused, as he sauntered to the bar.

A couple of Mexicans in black velvet and much silver courteously made way for him, and a fat and jolly bartender sloshed whisky into a ready glass. Slade downed his drink, called for another, and, as he toyed with it, casually scanned the reflections in the big mirror back of the bar.

One thing instantly attracted The Hawk's attention—the unusual quiet of the place. Men spoke in subdued voices that did not carry beyond their immediate neighborhood. The players at the tables placed their bets without unnecessary comment. The music of the really excellent orchestra was soft and seductive.

Even the feet of the dancers seemed to touch the floor lightly. The Hawk also noted that there was a litheness and leanness here that is lacking in rock busters and pick-and-shovel men.

Riders, nine out of ten of these jiggers, he told himself.

Range hands, or used to be range hands. Uhn-huh, Sliver was right, it's a salty gathering. But good at tending to their own business, I figure.

Slade finished his drink and sauntered to one of the tables ranged along the wall. As he sat down, a man came from behind the bar and started across the room toward the lunch counter, and The Hawk understood how the owner of the Branding Pen came by his nickname.

The man was powerfully built, with broad shoulders, a deep chest, and unusually long arms. But one leg was much shorter than its mate, and the discrepancy gave him a most peculiar gait. He would take a step, seem to hesitate, take a half step, and then a full-length stride.

Uhn-huh, "dot and carry", nodded Slade, thinking to himself. *That's just what it looks like he's doing.*

He got a good look at Carry's face as he passed under a light. It was a sinister-appearing face, heavy of jaw, bulging of forehead, with a tight gash of a mouth, and eyes that peered coldly from under shaggy brows. But to Walt Slade, old in experience with men—especially dangerous, despite his youthfulness of years—it seemed that the man's nose somewhat redeemed his unprepossessing face. It was a good straight nose, with something of the pleasant tip-tiltedness of a child's. It was the kind of a nose, Slade thought, that should have been set above a grin-quirked mouth and between twinkling eyes. This was decidedly not the case.

Just the same, that beak might be something to catch onto and hold onto, mused The Hawk, a speculative gleam in his clear eyes. *Yeah,* he nodded solemnly to himself, as a waiter hurried off for his order. *Yeah, I got a notion the big boss up topside of things usually leaves something he can reach down and get a good hold onto, no matter how botched up the job appears at first look.*

But when Carry Farr's cold eyes flickered in his direction and looked him over with a suspicious, calculating gaze accompanied by a grim hardening of the thin lips, The Hawk's dark brows drew together slightly, and the concentration furrow above the bridge of his high nose deepened.

Slade finished his really excellent meal, rolled a cigarette, and sauntered across the room to idle beside the Mexican orchestra. From time to time a young guitarist sang softly in a voice that was sweetly musical but lacked volume and made little impression. Absently he raised his gaze to the musician whose dark eyes brightened with recognition, and his teeth flashed in a smile. Impulsively he extended the guitar to Slade.

"*El capitán* weel seeng?" he asked persuasively.

Half smiling, Slade shook his head. But others had noted the Mexican's gesture.

"C'mon, feller, give us a song?" shouted a happy cowboy. He held a tiny girl in his long arms, her dark head coming hardly to his shoulder. She, too, smiled persuasively at the tall man who hesitated at the edge of the dance floor.

Other voices took it up, begging Slade to sing.

"You must be able to spout a good one, feller, if Mig asks you to," declared a brawny miner. "Don't be bashful!"

Walt Slade grinned, reached for the guitar, and swept his slim fingers across the strings. Then he threw back his black head and sang. He sang that old, old song of the Southwest, song of longing and heartache: "The Dove."

Men hushed their talk at the bar, turned, glass in hand, to stare at the singer whose voice rang through the room. The roulette wheel whirred to a halt, and nobody noticed where the bouncing ball had come to rest. A gambler laid down an ace-full, wrong side up, and left it that way.

With one accord the dancers stilled their steps and stood

motionless, the arms of the men still about the girls, and more than one pair of sinewy arms tightened their hold. Some of the girls tried to look careless. Others stared from eyes that were dampened by a mist of dead dreams. Some, including the tiny dark-haired dancer, let the tears fall unashamedly.

"If a white dove comes winging . . . ," pealed and rang and thundered the glorious baritone-bass. "Oh, entreat it to stay. . . ."

Dot 'n' Carry Farr stood behind his bar, great red hands resting on the shining surface, his hard face twisted. The hands tightened into iron-hard fists, and in the cold eyes was a stark misery as he stared at the singer, gloriously straight and tall as a young pine of the forest.

"For it is my soul, returning again to thee. . . ."

With a last whisper of melody and a crash of golden chords, song and music ended, and for a tense moment the room was utterly silent. Then a thunder of applause burst forth, dying slowly, abruptly stilling as a harsh voice rasped balefully: "Mighty purty! I wouldn't be s'prised, feller, if you could dance, too. C'mon, give us a coupla steps. C'mon! I ain't used to waitin' on purty boys when I tell 'em to do somethin'!"

The audience, engrossed in the song, had not noticed the hulking giant who had lunged through the swinging doors. He had lurched to the far end of the dance floor to stand, scowling blackly at the singer, his thick lips writhing back from big yellow teeth in a sneer. Blunt fingers of one enormous hand fingered the black butt of a heavy gun.

Walt Slade had noticed his entrance and had made a swift estimate of the new arrival. *Drunk!* he told himself. *Drunk and ugly, and plumb bad at any time.*

Now, however, he smiled at the speaker, even though his

eyes were no longer laughing, but the slate gray of stormy water. He shook his black head. "Nope, these boots got too high heels for dancin'," he declined.

A dance girl giggled; somebody sniggered beside the bar. The newcomer's face darkened still more; his lip lifted in a snarl.

"Yeah? Well, I'll jest shorten 'em a bit for you!"

The big blue gun seemed fairly to leap from its holster, the black muzzle jutting toward Walt Slade's feet.

From the guitar sounded a booming chord as Slade's slim fingers swept across the strings in a flashing blur of movement. In the crowded room a gun roared with a sodden hollowness. Then, still smoking, it flashed back into its holster, and the second chord of "Days of 'Forty-Nine," absolutely in tempo, boomed forth.

The giant at the end of the dance floor was reeling back, gripping at his streaming right hand. His gun, the lock smashed and battered by the heavy slug from Slade's Colt, slammed against the bar and *thudded* to the floor, yards distant. Through the booming chords of the guitar, Slade's voice sounded clear as falling water, deadly as the hiss of a rapier's blade.

"Don't reach for t'other one. I might miss the next time, and I always miss *inside* a feller's gun hand!"

The big man did not reach for his second gun. He was too white and sick for that. A .45 slug through the hand is no light matter. He reeled drunkenly for a moment, steadied himself, and glared unbelievingly at the man who still stood impassively thrumming the guitar. Once his mouth opened, and twice, but no words came forth. A third attempt, and his harsh voice, thickened by pain and fury, growled across the room: "This ain't finished, damn you!"

He wheeled and lurched through the swinging doors,

blood dripping to the floor in a steady stream. The night swallowed him, and a babbling whirl of words filled the room.

"Gawd! What shootin'! Crony had his hawgleg out 'n' lined!"

"And that feller never even stopped playin' his guitar!"

"And did you get that 'bout missin' *inside* t'other feller's gun hand? I'd hate like hell to have him miss me thataway! Who the hell is he, anyhow?"

"Sa-a-ay, don't that feller look sorta like Curly Bill Brocius over to Tombstone way? Big, black-headed, eyes like. . . ."

"Shet up! Curly Bill's s'posed to be dead! If he ain't, I figger he wouldn't hanker to have folks blabbin' out loud 'bout it."

"Right! I shore don't hanker to be doin' somethin' Curly Bill wouldn't hanker to have done, even if he is dead!"

Apparently heedless of the babble, Walt Slade handed the guitar to its owner.

"Who was that nice feller what just left?" he asked.

"That was the *Señor* Park Crony. He ees the foreman for the great *Señor* Hunter's Last Nugget Mine. *¡Muy malo hombre!*"

Slade was willing to agree that Crony was, indeed, a "very bad man." He turned, as a harsh voice spoke behind him, and looked into the sinister face of Carry Farr, owner of the saloon.

"I'd like to talk to you a minute, feller," said Farr, "in my back room. I got a hunch it'll sorta be to your interest to come along and gab with me a spell," he added with meaning.

Walt Slade gave him a keen glance, and nodded. Silently he followed the saloonkeeper, who led the way to the back room at his grotesque, sidling gait.

"Who the hell is he?" a voice demanded querulously as Slade closed the door after him.

There was a general shaking of heads. Miguel, the young guitarist, who might have enlightened them somewhat, smiled enigmatically, and held his peace.

III

"STOLEN GOLD"

At the moment the door closed behind Walt Slade, another man was riding into town. He was a blocky, sturdily built old man with hard, intolerant eyes peering from under shaggy brows. He had a mouth and jaw that promised a plentiful supply of that delightful quality called firmness in the fellow that's doing the talking and mule-headed stubbornness in other folks.

He sat his horse in an uncompromising fashion and gripped the reins as if he expected the cayuse to bolt at any moment and was prepared to bring him up short before he got away with any damned foolishness. He was powdered from head to foot with dust and appeared to be in anything but a pleasant humor. Even the big nickel-plated star on the left breast of his sagging vest winked balefully in the moonlight.

The rider did not pause at the Branding Pen, although, in passing, he glared at it as if the saloon were a personal affront. He rode farther up the street and pulled his tired horse to a halt in front of a bigger, brighter, more elegantly appointed establishment.

With a grunt he swung to the ground and bellowed an

order to a hanger-on nearby, who came forward obsequiously to lead the horse to a stable. With another grunt, that apparently held some meaning for the grunter, the old man entered the saloon, blinking owlishly in the glare of light.

"Hi, you, Sheriff!" called a voice. "C'mon over and set."

With a third grunt, which verged on a snort, the sheriff stumped solidly across the big and busy room and sat down at a table occupied by two other men.

"Hi, you, John, hi, you, Hunter!" he rumbled, reaching for a glass a waiter instantly placed at his elbow.

"Any luck, Wyatt?" asked the man who had called the invitation.

Sheriff Wyatt Cole snorted like a stallion with a burr under his tail. His face wrinkled with anger and disgust. He glowered at the speaker.

"Tryin' to be funny, John?" he demanded. "I didn't bring nobody back with me, did I?"

Old John Mosby, owner of the big Comstock Mine, twinkled his shrewd eyes.

"I've known you to have plenty of luck in a manhunt and not bring anybody back with you," he remarked softly.

The sheriff grunted in a mollified tone.

"Well, I didn't," he growled. "I didn't bring the hellions back, and I didn't leave none of 'em out in the desert or up in the hills, either. Didn't see hide nor hair of 'em. I went with Short and the boys 'round to the south by the water holes. Then I cut through the hills by way of the Cholla Trail and came out through Dry Water Cañon. Mebbe the boys had some luck, but I ain't very hopeful."

"Deputy Short and the posse got in a coupla hours back," remarked the second man at the table.

Sheriff Cole glared at the speaker, glowering from under his grizzled tufts.

Howard Hunter was an extremely handsome man with yellow hair inclined to curl and worn slightly long, snapping eyes of clear blue and regular features. He was lean and broad-shouldered, slim of hips and waist, in marked contrast to the blocky sheriff and the squat, ungainly owner of the Comstock Mine.

"They would," disapproved the sheriff.

Old John Mosby's round face suddenly darkened with anger. He hit the table a resounding blow with a fist like an over-smoked ham.

"Somethin's gotta be done!" he declared. "You realize this makes three gold shipments we lost inside of a year? Nigh onto thirty thousand dollars this time, and two good men killed, and Hank Givens, the stage driver, hoverin' 'tween life and death right this minute. If Doc Preston pulls him through, it'll be a plumb miracle! I tell you somethin's gotta be done about these damn' Dawn Riders. Who the hell ever give them that fool name, anyhow?"

"It's 'cause they always do their work jest before sunrise, when it's darkest and folks is sleepiest and most liable to be sorta off guard," said the sheriff. "I reckon them two shotgun guards was snatchin' forty winks about then and woke up with harps or shovels in their hands. It was some salty hold-up, all right, jest almost as the stage was pullin' into Harding. 'Nother fifteen minutes and that shipment would 'a' been on the train and safe. I figger the Limited must've been passin' right by while they was doin' their dirty work."

Old John swore in his hairy throat.

Howard Hunter leaned forward interestedly. "Neither of the guards lived long enough to give a description of the outfit?" he asked.

"Hell, no," grumbled the sheriff. "They was drilled

plumb center. It's a miracle that old Hank Givens was alive to say anythin'. He told Doc Preston jest before he passed out that the leader fella of the outfit leaned outta his hull, while he was layin' on the ground with a smashed shoulder and a busted leg, and shoved a gun against his head and pulled the trigger.

"Was one of them funny things what sometimes happens. Hank looked like he'd been drilled plumb between the eyes, but I reckon the gun was held at a sorta off angle. Anyway, the bullet scooted along the bone, jest under the skin, and come out jest over Hank's left ear instead of goin' through his head.

"Hank told Doc that the leader feller was a tall *hombre* with black hair and black whiskers comin' almost up to his eyes, as usual. Said the eyes was mighty bad-lookin'. Reckon they would look that way to a feller what was lookin' into 'em over the wrong end of a gun. He said the rest of the gang appeared to be mostly Mexicans."

"Black whiskers growin' almost up to his eyes," mused Hunter. "Appears to me a feller lookin' like that oughtn't to be so hard to spot."

The sheriff shook his head and grunted. "Whiskers and hair is too easy to grow in a coupla weeks of keepin' outta sight," he said. "Chances are, next time anybody sees that gunslingin' gent, he'll be clean-shaved and have his hair trimmed, and Mexicans ain't always the Mexicans they look to be.

"Jest the same," he added with a vicious snap, "I'm gonna keep a plumb close eye on that greaser hang-out run by Carry Farr. Plenty of Mexicans there and plenty of shady characters there, too, or I miss my guess a heap. That damn' dump had oughta be closed up. This town needs less places like that and more like Howard's Cattlemen's Club here."

He glanced around the well-filled, comparatively quiet room as he spoke, his eyes appreciating the orderly arrangements, the shining glassware, the well-stocked back-bar.

"I'm gonna wash up before I eat," he said, levering his bulky body from the chair. "See you in a minute."

Old John Mosby studied his blocky figure as he stumped across the room.

"Somethin's gotta be done," he repeated. "It ain't only these stage robberies and the one at the bank. The wide-loopin' of high-grade ore outta my mine is even worse, from my way of lookin' at it. Production has fell off a full thirty percent in the past six months. I've tried every way I know to run the hellions down, and ain't had no luck.

"I put some fellers I plumb trusted to work in the mine 'longside the muckers and rock men. Result . . . two gets smashed flat 'neath a rock fall what had no business fallin'. One tumbles down a shaft where he hadn't oughta been, and 'nother's picked up in the alley back of that damn' Branding Pen rum hole with a knife in his back. No, it ain't so much the shipments I been losin'. What bothers me is the high-grade ore I'm losin'."

Howard Hunter's handsome face looked worried.

"Maybe it don't matter so much to you," he said, "but it matters plenty to me. My Last Nugget ain't no Comstock, and what I lost outta them shipments hurt like hell."

Mosby nodded, glancing about the busy saloon.

"You got a payin' proposition here," he remarked with apparent irrelevancy.

"Damn' lucky for me I have," growled Hunter. "If it wasn't for the Cattlemen's Club, the Last Nugget would jest about be closin' down after this last raid. Uhn-huh, you're right, John, somethin's gotta be done."

Mosby glanced in the direction of the washroom, saw

nothing of the sheriff, and lowered his voice.

"I'm doin' somethin'," he remarked sententiously. "Wyatt's a nice feller, but he's gettin' old, and I figger sorta losin' his grip. I wouldn't want him to know what I'm tellin' you, 'cause I wouldn't wanna hurt his feelin's. I sent a letter to Cap McNelty of the Rangers, week before last, askin' him to send a coupla men over here."

"The hell you did! What'd McNelty say?"

Old John snorted his anger and disgust.

"Wrote me he couldn't very well spare any men right now, what with the trouble along the border over to the west, and such. Said he'd detail a man or two to this district sometime next month, if possible. Said the matter concerned was something for the local authorities to handle, so far as he could make out, but he'd lend a hand when he could. Helluva note! But, mebbe, this last robbin' and killin' may make him stir his stumps a little. Forget it now, here comes Wyatt."

Just as the sheriff was knifing a final stab of pie under his mustache, a huge man entered the saloon and came slouching across the room to the table. His face was twisted with pain and his right hand, elaborately bandaged, was suspended in a sling.

Howard Hunter stared at him in amazement.

"What the hell happened to you, Crony?" he demanded.

The big man slumped into a chair and growled an order to a waiter.

"Feller shot me," he rumbled.

Now both the sheriff and Hunter stared.

"You mean to tell me," sputtered the former, "that somebody busted your gun hand with a slug?"

Park Crony muttered and gurgled through his drink

39

what was evidently intended for assent.

"Slip up behind you, or somethin'?" Hunter asked quietly.

Crony set down his glass and glared.

"I got my faults, boss," he rumbled. "Plenty of 'em, and I ain't denyin' it. But lyin' ain't one of 'em, that is leastwise except where there ain't no helpin' it. I ain't gonna tell no fancy highfalutin' yarn about how this jigger got me at a disadvantage or somethin' like that. He jest nacherly pulled so fast that he blowed my hawgleg outta my hand 'fore I could crook a finger."

The sheriff made a noise like a rooster with its crop too full. Hunter leaned forward, his blue eyes glittering.

"Suppose you start at the beginnin'," he suggested.

Crony grunted, and ordered another drink.

"I was drunk," he prefaced.

"That's not news," Hunter interrupted sarcastically.

"I don't drink durin' workin' hours . . . any of 'em!" Crony blazed. He glared hot resentment at his employer, but his angry gaze wavered and shifted before Hunter's cold, blue glitter. "Yeah, I was drunk," he repeated, "but not so's I couldn't handle myself. You know, when I gets drunk, I gets sorta playful."

The sheriff's snort interrupted, and after a fragmentary mumble about "barb-wired bulls with burrs under their tails," Crony went on talking. "I was feelin' playful, and sorta outta sorts, when I ambled into that rum hole of Carry Farr's. There was a feller with black hair, and the kinda eyelashes what are a inch long and looks like they been dusted with soot.

"He was playin' a guitar and singin' a Mex song. I didn't like him. Reckon he was too damn' purty or somethin', with them snappin' eyes and that hawk nose. I took a notion it'd be sorta nice to have him give the outfit a bullet dance.

"Well, it didn't work! I had my hawgleg in my hand and was jest throwin' down on one of his fancy high heels when that gun comes out and throws down, and it waren't no use. Before I could pull trigger, my iron was halfway across the room and my hand busted all to hell. And that damn' hellion never even stopped playin' his infernal guitar!"

"That god-damned Brandin' Pen!" swore the sheriff. "All the owlhoots in this end of Texas hole up there. Someday I'm gonna bust that horned toad corral so wide open you can drive a six-hoss stage through it and not scrape a wheel hub!"

Howard Hunter leaned forward, his blue eyes sparkling with interest.

"That feller," he prompted, "was he sort of tall, wide in the shoulder, with gray eyes?"

"Don't know what color his damn' eyes was," growled Crony, "but when they're lookin' through powder smoke, they're bad, damn' bad! Yeah, he's a sorta big hellion, come to think of it. Not more'n a patch on my back when it comes to size, but purty big in ordinary considerin's. Why?"

Hunter sat back, his eyes thoughtful.

"I've heard tell of that jigger," he said. "He's been ridin' through southwest Texas for quite a spell now. Always seems to be nearabouts when somethin' particularly off-color and salty is pulled, but ain't never had nothin' tied to him, so far as I ever heard tell. Associates with Mexicans a lot. They call him El Halcón. That's The Hawk in Mex. Goes around with a guitar slung over his shoulder and sings while he rides. Rides one helluva fine black cayuse."

Old John Mosby glanced shrewdly at the speaker.

"Hmm," he said. "Fellers what saw 'em say them damn' Dawn Riders fork black cayuses, particularly the hellion what seems to boss the outfit."

"All hosses look black in early mornin', jest before it gets light," the sheriff pointed out. "That is all exceptin' white or gray bronc's, and I ain't never heard of such an outfit goin' in for ghost-colored hosses. Jest the same, John," he added with a speculative gleam in his eyes, "it's worth thinkin' on."

IV

"THE DAWN RIDERS"

In the back room of the Branding Pen, Carry Farr waved Slade to a chair.

"Set," he invited. "I done ordered a bottle of my private stock sent in. It's got more snake poison and cactus juice in it than what I shove across the bar."

"Uhn-huh, a lot milder'n the ordinary run," Slade conceded gravely, after sampling the bottle that a waiter had placed on the table. "You need bigger glasses for this brand. Can't hardly get the taste otherwise."

"You're shore copper-lined," Farr declared admiringly. "Shet the door after you, Clem," he said to the waiter.

After the waiter had gone, Carry Farr wiped his mouth with the back of a hairy hand and stared across the table.

"Feller," he said softly, " 'pears to me your face is sorta familiar." He held up his hand as Slade stiffened slightly.

"Ain't aimin' to do no pryin' into other folks' affairs," he said, "but I got a good memory for faces, particularly if I've happened to see them through gunsmoke. You see, I used to put in some time over Franklin way in El Paso County. And I happened to be in town the time that bank job was pulled off in Holman, and they had the big street fight. I was standin' 'cross the street in Buster's hardware store, and I recollect the feller in front of the bank who. . . ."

"I reckon we can do without any more gabbin' about that," Slade interrupted quietly.

Carry Farr glanced at the gray eyes back of the dark lashes, and nodded.

"I was jest aimin' to show that I do know who you are, feller," he said with pointed emphasis. "Don't worry, I got a reputation for keepin' my lip buttoned. What I'm gettin' at is this . . . I got a pretty good notion why you're here, and I wanted to point out that a feller can't go doin' nothin' without causin' folks to talk. And if a feller gets him a job on a spread 'round 'bout town, he ain't got much time for anythin' else. That's why I said out in t'other room it'd be to your interest to have a talk with me. Now listen. . . ."

It was in the dead, dark hours just before the dawn that Walt Slade made his way back to his little room in the livery stable on the outskirts of town. He was just turning toward the door when there came to his ears a soft drumming. He located it as coming from the trail that ran from south to north. The trail turned sharply at the edge of the town to writhe through gloomy, mysterious Dry Water Cañon and wind on into the bleak fastnesses of the Cholla Hills.

Louder grew the sound, beating swiftly from the south. Slade focused his eyes on a gray fragment on the trail that could be seen from where he stood. It shimmered faintly in the starlight, empty, lonely.

Then abruptly it was no longer empty. Huge, dark shapes, distorted and magnified by the illusive light, were drifting swiftly across the patch of gray like the ghosts of long-dead dawns. As fantastically as they had appeared, they vanished, and only that hollow drumming was left to speak of their passing, a drumming that swiftly faded to a whisper of sound that died in the shadows to the west.

When Slade got up late in the morning, Sliver Oakes was already about. Slade thought it wise to tell him of his new status. He was a little surprised at the way Sliver took it.

"You gotta pay in advance, after all!" squealed Sliver Oakes. "Any young hellion what takes such a job as shotgun guard in a hell-hooten hole like Carry Farr's Brandin' Pen ain't to be relied on to be here to pay his feed and room bill when it comes due. Collectin' from estates is too damn' much trouble!"

Walt Slade, standing tall and lithe in the blaze of the noontime sun, chuckled as his merry eyes ran over the excited fat man.

"What's wrong with the Brandin' Pen?" he wanted to know.

"Oh, nothin', nothin' at all!" Sliver replied sarcastically. "The Sunday school and prayer meetin's clutter it up awful, but t'otherwise she's fine. Nice place! Why, fellers has been knowed to stay alive for 'most as long as two hours! Such a nice, gentled outfit of hoss thieves and wide-loopers and owlhoots bed down there in perfect peace and get along with the sidewinders and Gila monsters and vinegaroons and tarantulas what have been chased outta the desert 'cause they was too damn' ornery to be allowed to associate with the other varmints!

"Nice place! Shootin' in there last night, as per usual. I heard tell, somebody blowed a gun outta Park Crony's hand and laid Park up for a month. Figger that's a damn' lie, though. There ain't but one man in this section of Texas what can shade Park with a gun."

Slade looked up. "Who's that man?" he asked with interest.

"Howard Hunter, who owns the Last Nugget Mine. Crony works for him as head foreman there. I calculate Hunter to be the fastest gun hand in the state, outside mebbe of that big feller, Jim Hatfield, of the Rangers. Gentleman . . . Hunter. Tends to his own business and is plumb respectable, but plumb salty when necessary. He owns the Cattleman's Club, swellest saloon in town. Barkeeps actually wear collars and shave twice a week. Almighty different place from that damn' Brandin' Pen, and Hunter's mighty different from Carry Farr."

"And, besides ownin' the Brandin' Pen, what's the matter with Farr?" The Hawk asked.

Sliver Oakes shrugged. "Can't say as they's anythin' definite," he admitted. "Mexicans like him, and so does most fellers what ain't gettin' along any too well or what's had trouble. Old Doc Preston swears he's worth a dozen Hunters and even a couple of John Mosbys, 'spite the fact that Doc and Mosby, who owns the big Comstock Mine, is purty good friends. But, then, old Doc is sorta queer . . . hipped with book larnin', I reckon, and mebbe teched in the head a little in consequence.

"Fact is, they's too many salty hellions from both sides the line hang out in Carry's place and on good terms with him. I ain't one to truck talk I ain't shore 'bout, and what I'm tellin' you now ain't no personal 'pinion of mine."

He glanced around and lowered his voice.

"There's folks what believe Carry Farr might be the big boss of the Dawn Riders, and Sheriff Cole is sorta one of 'em, though he ain't never been able to prove nothin' on Carry."

"The Dawn Riders? What the blazes are they?"

Again Oakes glanced about nervously, although there was no one in sight, and Slade noted curiously that his fat face was beaded with sweat. Sliver lowered his voice still more.

"They ain't been a salty owlhoot job pulled off in this district for the past year but what the Dawn Riders has been into it," he said. "Nobody knows who they are, and folks what has been overcurious ain't 'joyed particular good health.

"There was old man Chisum, who lost a big herd last year and got a posse of his riders together and set out after the Dawn Riders. Was pressin' 'em sorta hard, I figger, when all of a sudden the trail in the snow jest stopped all to once. Of course, it was an old trick. The outfit jest doubled back careful to a thicket, brushed out their tracks into the thicket, and laid low.

"But they did it so almighty slick that Chisum and his bunch was plumb throwed off guard for a minute. There him and his dozen Solomons was, tryin' to figger out what had happened, bunched up and showin' hard and clear 'gainst a white cliff."

Sliver paused to roll a cigarette. Slade waited expectantly.

"Two of the Chisum boys lived long enough to tell what happened," Sliver concluded succinctly.

Walt Slade nodded thoughtfully. "Salty outfit, all right," he admitted, a cold and retrospective gleam in his gray eyes.

"They always work jest 'fore it gets light. That's how they come by their name," Sliver went on. "Jest last week they held up the Harding stage 'fore it hit town and ran off with the Comstock and Last Nugget bullion shipments.

"Sheriff's been chasin' hisself 'round the county ever since, but ain't got nothin' to show for it but corns under the seat of his pants. Reckon he'll take to ridin' herd on Carry Farr and the Brandin' Pen for a spell again, and, meanwhile, the Dawn Riders'll pull another job."

"Farr's a lame man," Slade pointed out. "Don't look like a man with one leg shorter than t'other could get by without bein' noticed."

"That brings out a funny thing about the feller what bosses the outfit," said Sliver. "Ain't nobody ever seen him outta his saddle. His men do all the work what's necessary, and he sits up top his hull and watches. Lends a hand from there, if necessary, but never comes down off his hoss to help on the ground.

"Why, in that last stage hold-up, he plugged the driver while old Hank was layin' on the ground. Leaned over and leaned way down. Didn't unfork like a feller naturally would for a job he wanted to make shore of. Reckon that's what kept old Hank alive. Bullet sorta skidded and didn't go through his head like it would 'a' if the gun had been held plumb straight instead of off center.

" 'Feller is always husky-looking, like Carry looks on a hoss, and has black hair, like what Carry's got, and wears black whiskers like what Carry could grow if necessary."

"Takes time to grow whiskers," Slade said.

"Uhn-huh, and Carry Farr's always been the sorta feller what keeps to hisself a lot. Goes off alone, and the like. Sometimes he ain't 'round for coupla weeks or more. Cook, the head barkeep, runs the place when Carry ain't there, and does a good job of runnin' it, too. But, hell! I'm talkin' like I was makin' out a case 'gainst Carry, which I shore ain't aimin' to. Fact is, I sorta like the hoppety-skip hellion, but there's plenty of fellers what don't, includin' the sheriff. And no wonder! Carry's place has caused him plenty of gray hairs.

"Jest last week there was a regular heller of a row in there. Ended up with the shotgun guard plugged 'tween the eyes and a hellion they didn't nobody know with a charge of buckshot where his insides had oughta been. Incidentally, that's the third guard what's cashed in his chips in the past six months."

This remark, made in a significant tone of voice, ended the conversation, except that Sliver profanely declined the payment in advance which Slade proffered with vast solemnity.

V

"SHOTGUN GUARD"

Mingling with the frankly lawless element, the reckless cowboys, and the trouble-hunting miners who frequented the Branding Pen, Walt Slade took up his new duties peacefully and serenely. Unlike his predecessors, who were now riding herd on the Milky Way, he dispensed with the high look-out chair and the clumsy shotgun. Lithe, alert, he mixed with the crowd, seeing everything while apparently paying scant attention to anything. The first few nights were slightly strenuous, but after that the Branding Pen cooled down considerably.

Slade didn't actually have to kill anybody, but several trouble-seeking gents were punctured, more or less seriously, while some others nursed discolored eyes and noses that had suddenly attained remarkable prominence and a pronounced change of shape.

"I run straight games," Carry Farr had told his new hand on his first night of duty, "and I want 'em kept straight.

Take your regular house cut and you come out more ahead in the end than if you trim the suckers with crooked wheels and dealin' and such. Trim 'em and they don't come back. Treat 'em square and they do. But it ain't easy to keep the dealers from pullin' somethin' now and then."

Slade had nodded, and kept his eyes open. A little later he spotted a dealer making a deck change spots and color.

Gettin' himself a little private cut, Slade had mused.

He had had a waiter call the dealer aside. Quietly he had told him what he had seen and suggested that he cut it out. The dealer, a big man with a hard jaw and truculent eyes, had glowered at Slade, and his face had flushed darkly.

"I know my business," he had spat, "and I don't need no damn' look-out to tell it to me."

One-fifteenth of a second later he had sat down on the floor, and sat down hard. Slade had taken him by the collar and the seat of the pants and had thrown him through a window without waiting to open it. The gambler had opened it on his way out.

He had come back by way of the door, streaming blood from a score of cuts, a gun in one hand and a knife in the other. Slade had shot the gun from his hand, taken the knife away from him, and had sent him out again—via the window. That time he had stayed out.

This bit of by-play had been noticed by the other dealers, and very quickly the word got around town that the games at the Branding Pen were straight without reservations. As a result, business improved.

"Why, there's even fellers what used to go no place but to Hunter's swell Cattleman's Club settin' in our games now," chuckled Carry Farr. "And look at old man Ward of the C Bar Q buckin' the wheel over there. He'll toss away the price of fifty beef critters in a evenin' and think nothin' of it. Take a busted nickel off him crooked and he'll shoot the lights out!"

Sliver Oakes snorted at the stories that came his way.

"Yeah, you're gettin' a reputation, all right," he squeaked to Slade. "And," he added darkly, "that's jest what'll be your finish. Salty jiggers are goin' to hear about you and set out to get themselves a reputation by downin' you. Jest pay mind to what I tell you, and see if I ain't right."

Three days after taking the job at the Branding Pen, Slade encountered Sheriff Wyatt Cole. Slade and Carry Farr were strolling along the main street before going to the saloon for the evening session. They paused in front of the bank. A mule cart, guarded by two watchful individuals with sawed-off shotguns, stood at the curb. From it men were carrying ingots of metal into the bank. The ingots were evidently surprisingly heavy for their size.

"It's the monthly clean-up of the Lost Nugget, Hunter's mine," explained Farr, who recognized the cart and its driver. "Coupla months' clean-up, for that matter, I understand. Them fellers what robbed the Harding stage last week missed the Lost Nugget's big shipment. Hunter only had a little one in that batch, comparatively speakin', but the Comstock had a whopper."

Slade eyed the ingots curiously. "How many mines does Hunter own?" he asked.

"Jest the one," replied Farr. "It's a purty good vein of ore, but not up to the Comstock's. Hunter's makin' some money above operatin' expenses, which are purty heavy, I reckon. But old John Mosby's gettin' rich outta the Comstock, or was 'fore he commenced losin' so much high-grade ore."

"How's that?"

"Hell, nobody knows. Mosby swears he's bein' robbed

right and left, but he ain't never been able to pin the stealin' on anybody. You see, the Comstock vein is one of them spotty lodes that runs along average for a spell and then all of a sudden runs high-grade. They ain't no way to tell when the high-grade is gonna show.

"The high-grade has always been what made the Comstock a rich mine. All of a sudden, about six months ago, the high-grade stopped showin' at the stamp mill, or showed mighty scarce. Mosby swears somebody's stealin' high-grade outta the mine. He's an old-time minin' man and knows about all there is to know about the business. He says the high-grade wouldn't naturally peter out and the vein still hold regular every other way.

"He's plumb convinced somebody is wide loopin' his ore, but he ain't never been able to catch anybody doin' it. Of course, the Comstock is a big mine with purt' nigh onto a thousand men on its payroll, which makes it sorta hard to check.

"Big mystery is how they get the ore outta the mine or grab it before it gets to the mill. It's got old John and the sheriff damn' nigh loco. Here comes the sheriff right now, incidentally. Figgered he'd be showin' up soon."

"Is there another mine close to the Comstock that the ore might be run into from the Comstock tunnels?"

"Hell, no," grunted Farr. "The Last Nugget is the only other diggin' in this particular section. All the other mines are 'way over to the east side of the hills. And the Last Nugget tunnels don't anywhere come within a mile of the Comstock. Mosby and Hunter figgered that angle and tossed it out. You can't dig a tunnel a mile long without attractin' attention."

Slade continued to stare at the ingots, the furrow between his gray eyes deepening. He glanced up as Sheriff Cole halted and glowered at him and Farr with scant friendliness.

Farr nodded, and the sheriff acknowledged the greeting with a stiff jerk of his head. His choleric old eyes went over Slade from head to foot. The Hawk's amused gaze, that met his suspicious stare unwaveringly, plainly irked the sheriff.

"Feller, what'd you do last afore you took to workin' in that hell hole up the street? And how come you to pick on this town for a stoppin' point?" he demanded.

Slade's gray eyes danced and the corners of his rather wide mouth quirked upward. He countered with a question of his own.

"Where's the other twelve fellers?"

"What? What the hell?" demanded the bewildered sheriff.

"You see, it's this way," Slade explained confidentially, "the last time I was asked a lot of questions, there was twelve fellers sittin' alongside in a box listenin'."

The sheriff stared for a moment, then his blocky face turned fiery red as he got the meaning. He gurgled in his throat, snapped at his mustache, and seemed about to explode. With a mighty effort he mastered his indignation, but his eyes remained red.

"You watch your step, you impudent whippersnapper, or it won't be the last time there's a jury listenin' to you answerin' questions," he fumed. "I got my eyes on you . . . on both of you hellions . . . and don't forget it!"

He stormed into the bank in the wake of the last ingot. Slade and Farr passed on up the street, the former chuckling. Farr, however, was serious.

"There ain't no use in gettin' the old jigger all hopped up 'gainst you," he remonstrated. "You're walkin' a mighty narrow ridge hereabouts as it is, without goin' outta your way to look for trouble."

"Lookin' for trouble is sometimes the best way not to find it," Slade replied enigmatically. "I wonder when the Comstock Mine sends a shipment to the bank?"

"They oughta be runnin' one down from the mills tomorrow afternoon about this time," Farr replied. "The bank 'most always sends a shipment to Harding on the first of the month, and that's the day after tomorrow."

He cast a questioning glance at his companion, but Slade offered no further comment. Farr grunted and "dotted" his way to the saloon alongside Slade.

Slade strolled past the bank the following afternoon as the Comstock clean-up was being carried into the vault. He did not pause, but he eyed the big ingots with keen interest. Very thoughtfully, he made his way to the Branding Pen, and for some time he sat in the little back room, his black brows drawn together, his gray eyes somber.

Carry Farr limped in and handed out a piece of news.

"I heard tell they're sendin' six outriders with the stage when she heads for Harding tomorrow. Reckon Mosby and Hunter ain't takin' any chances with that big shipment. The Dawn Riders'll get a bellyful if they tackle that outfit. Old Jim Kirk, who used to be a buffalo hunter, is goin' along with his old Sharps Fifty, and there's Sam Simon and some more of that sort. Yeah, I reckon that shipment is gonna make the railroad for shore."

Slade nodded absently. A little later, after a few minutes of precise conversation with Farr, he entered the saloon.

It was a busy night, a number of riders from the big ranches to the east being in town. There was also, Slade noted, more than the usual sprinkling of quiet, cool-eyed individuals who drank warily and played the games in silence.

The crowd was orderly, however, and the shotgun guard found little to do. It was well after midnight when he casually sauntered into the little back room and closed the door behind him.

Carry Farr was seated at the table. He looked up expectantly as Slade entered. A meal for two was on the table, but Farr was not eating.

"OK," he told Slade. "I've give orders to let us alone while we're eatin'. Oughta give an hour or so without any interruptions, barrin' a bad fight startin' out there."

"Things are quiet," Slade replied crisply. "Too damn' quiet," he added, hitching his cartridge belts a trifle higher. "Makes me wonder."

With a nod to Farr, he passed across the room. As he reached the door that led to the alley back of the saloon, Farr blew out the lamp. Slade slipped out and closed the door behind him. He did not wait to see the faint pencil of light that showed Carry had re-lighted the lamp, but glided noiselessly down the alley.

He turned into a quiet side street, followed it a little way, and slipped into another alley. A few minutes later he brought up in the rear of a building rather more substantial than its fellows, the building that housed the Miners and Cattlemen's Bank.

VI

"GUNS IN THE DARK"

Rats gnawing their way through a baseboard might have made the small sound Walt Slade could hear inside the bank. It was a persistent sound, never varying, a thin, little sound, with something gratingly metallic about it. The Hawk listened intently for a moment, then gradually straightened up to peer through the window beneath which he crouched.

That window should have been locked, but it wasn't. There was an opening an inch or so in width between the sash and the sill. With a movement so slowly careful as to be almost imperceptible, Slade shoved his slim fingers through the opening, gripped the sash firmly, and pressed upward. Responding to that steady, perfectly controlled pressure, the window rose without a sound. The queer, persistent gnawing became more distinct.

Peering with narrowed eyes, The Hawk could make out a rectangle of lighter shadow that he knew to be a doorway. Beyond was a faint, diffused glow. Levering his body up on rigid forearms, he performed the seemingly impossible feat of swinging both legs over the sill.

The veins stood out on his forehead like cords with the strain as he eased his feet to the floor without a sound. Inside the back room of the bank he stood up, and for a wavering second of time his tall form was outlined against the faint glow beyond the open door. In that tense instant he heard a sound.

It was but the dry creak of saddle leather, barely perceptible, as a mounted man shifted his weight ever so slightly. But it was enough to save The Hawk's life. Instantly he was going sideways and down from the window square. He was on hands and toes below the sill when the *screeching* slug slammed the glass of the upper pane to fragments. Outside the bank a gun cracked with the nerve-shattering unexpectedness of a thunderclap in a snowstorm.

A numbed silence followed the report. Then the dark building erupted into a weird pandemonium of action. The room seemed fairly to explode with the roar of six-shooters. Metal crashed to the floor. Curses spat through the air. Red flashes stabbed the gloom, and bullets chunked and *thudded* against the walls.

Weaving, ducking, shifting, Walt Slade answered those red flashes lancing from the inner room. The *boom* of his big guns blended in a drum roll of sound.

A man screamed shrilly, the high-pitched screech knifing the very zenith of agony and chopping off short in a bubbling grunt. There was the *thud* of a body falling to the floor, then a terrific crashing of glass.

Guns jutting forward, Slade leaped for the inner room as a blast of cool air poured through the swirls of powder smoke. A bull's-eye lantern lay on its side on the floor, the flickering beam falling across a jumble of tools before the dark loom of the bank vault. Still sticking in the vault door was the slim drill that had made that faint rat-gnawing as it had bitten into the stubborn steel.

There was a bundle of stout buckskin bags, and beside them the body of a man. The window across the room was a jagged hanging of splintered frame and shattered glass. Even as The Hawk reached it, hoof beats *crackled,* driving swiftly away from the bank.

Shouts were echoing the hoof beats, drawing nearer, and the pad of hurrying boots. Slade hesitated an instant, sweeping the room with a penetrating, all-embracing glance. He jerked the dead man into the beam of the lantern, stared into his distorted face an instant, and grunted with disappointment.

Then he went across the back room like a shadow, dived through the open window, and lit running. He darted along the dark alleys as yells and curses boomed in front of the bank.

Scant minutes later he tapped lightly on the back door of the Branding Pen. He heard Carry Farr extinguish the light and hurry to unlock the door. He slipped in. Farr re-lighted the lamp, and The Hawk sat down at the table, jerked open a drawer, and, hauling out brushes, rags, and oil, began cleaning his guns.

"No luck," he replied tersely to Farr's question. "They beat me to it. Look-out who must've been under cover mighty slick spotted me as I eased through a window and damn' near plugged me. I shot it out with three fellers inside the bank workin' on the vault door, downed one of 'em, and the other two went through the window.

"Got a good look at the hellion that cashed in. Never saw his face before. Didn't get more'n a flickering squint at the other two. All I saw was gun flashes and black whiskers. Here, shove these dirty rags and the brush and oil up the chimney over there. Can't afford to take any chances.

"Wyatt Cole's the kinda jigger who's liable to pop in any minute and ask to take a look at our guns. He's already got us tagged in his head as owlhoot members, or I'm a heap mistaken. Let's eat, and send for some hot coffee."

Farr opened the inner door and called to a waiter to bring the coffee. Then he and Slade proceeded to eat a leisurely dinner. They were enjoying the steaming coffee when a commotion sounded in the saloon.

A moment later Sheriff Wyatt Cole banged open the door and stood glowering, his head outthrust, brawny hands clamped on the butts of his guns. Beside him stood two deputies with cocked rifles. Looking over the stocky sheriff's head was Howard Hunter, a sardonic light in his glittering blue eyes.

"Howdy, Sheriff," greeted Walt Slade, apparently oblivious to the menace of rifle and six-gun, "come and have some coffee. Sorta chilly out tonight, isn't it?"

As the sheriff stood gurgling in outraged dignity, Carry Farr levered his crippled body erect.

"What the hell's the idea?" he demanded indignantly. "This is a private room. What do you mean by bustin' in here like you was figgerin' on stagin' a hold-up?"

He glared at the sheriff and his deputies.

The deputies shifted their feet uncomfortably. One surreptitiously lowered the hammer of his rifle.

"Somebody jest tried to burgle the bank!" blurted the sheriff.

"Well, what the hell you comin' here for? This ain't the bank!"

With a visible effort the sheriff controlled his temper.

"Listen, Farr," he said quietly, "I ain't aimin' to be persecutin' nobody, but I'm an officer of the law, elected by the people of this county and sworn to do my duty. I'm doin' it as I see it, that's why I'm comin' here tonight.

"There was shootin' at the bank, plenty of it, and they's a dead man layin' in there alongside a kit of burglar tools, and they's blood spots in the alley outside the bank, which goes to show another gent or two got punctured in the shindig. Likeways there was a feller heard runnin' up the alley back of your place right after the row down there ended.

"This feller, Slade, what's workin' for you is a new man here, and there's stories goin' 'round about him. I ain't sayin' they're true, and I ain't sayin' they even stick close to the real facts, but when things happen like what happened tonight, I can't overlook no bets."

He walked steadily across the room, his eyes never leaving Walt Slade.

"Feller," he said quietly, "I'd like to take a look at your guns."

His lips quirked slightly, Slade drew his Colts and laid them on the table. The sheriff picked one up, sniffed at it, glanced at the cylinder and inserted a tentative fingertip in the muzzle. With a grunt he laid the iron down and gave its fellow a similar once over. Shaking his head and muttering under his mustache, he placed the second gun on the table.

"OK, so far," he rumbled. "There ain't nothin' to show they've been shot tonight."

His glance traveled over The Hawk from head to foot, and again he shook his head. He was turning away when Howard Hunter sauntered forward, his blue eyes glittering.

"I jest happened to notice that Farr packs a coupla hawglegs, too," he remarked softly.

"Farr's a lame man," growled the sheriff as the saloonkeeper started angrily. "He couldn't've been the feller runnin' up the alley. It would take him all night to make that distance."

"But," interposed Hunter in his musical voice, "fellers have been known to trade guns at times, particularly when they didn't have time to clean their own."

"So that's what you're hintin' at, eh, you long-haired hellion!" grated Farr. "Here!"

He jerked his guns from their holsters and slammed them on the table. Almost apologetically the sheriff examined them. With a grunt of disgust he laid them down.

"You're always detectivin' somethin', Howard," he growled. "I figger you'd better stick to minin' and the liquor business. Peace officerin' jest naturally ain't in your line. C'mon, you fellows, let's be gettin' outta here."

With his two deputies at his heels, he stamped out of the room. Howard Hunter, however, lingered a moment. Standing beside the table, he looked Walt Slade squarely in the eyes, and laid on the table an exploded .45 cartridge.

"I picked up this shell, and a few more like it, in the alley back of the bank," he said softly. Standing the smoke streaked brass container on end, he tapped it with a tapering, sensitive finger. "The gun that shot it has a firin' pin that shore hits the cap a long way off center," he remarked in tones of casual conversation. "That firin' pin would sorta stand out in any company. Fact is, if I was the feller what owned that gun, I'd be travelin' away from this district right now, and travelin' fast."

His burning blue gaze had never left Slade's face. The Hawk sat rigidly, staring at him, lips slightly parted.

"Yeah, I'd shore be travelin', if I happened to be that feller," Hunter repeated.

Turning, he sauntered out of the room, closing the door after him, leaving Slade and Carry Farr staring at each other. After a long moment the latter spoke.

"Who'd've figgered that slick-faced hellion would be that smart?" he demanded. "Pickin' up them shells and noticin' that off-center markin' on the cap! But he allus did set hisself up as bein' mighty pert. He played smart when he first come to this district, and shore overplayed his hand. Cost him the Comstock Mine."

"How's that?" Slade asked with interest.

"Was this way. There waren't no town of Cholla in them days, five years or so back. Jest Harding, the railroad town over east. Fellers had been pickin' up specimens of gold bearin' float in the gullies and dry washes hereabout for quite a spell. Lots of 'em in Dry Water Cañon, where an almighty big stream of water must've come down at one time, jedgin' by all the signs. Hell knows where it come from . . . there ain't none there now."

Farr leaned back in his chair, getting comfortable.

"Prospectors kept comin' out from Harding to go over

this territory, but nobody had any real luck till Hunter and John Mosby come along. Mosby is a Texan, El Paso County, and in them days he didn't have a pot to cook in. Hunter come to Harding from somewheres over East. Talked lots more like an Eastern feller in them days. He knows the minin' business, all right, and is purty well educated, I take it.

"Him and Mosby set out from Harding together for the Cholla Hills. They waren't partners. Jest travelin' together till they got to the hills. There they figgered on splittin' up. Down at the mouth of the big dry wash south of here, they stopped to decide which way each would choose. Jest then a jack rabbit scooted out of a bush and went hightailin' up the wash to the left. Old John Mosby shore likes to tell that story from here on.

" 'There's a sign, Hunter,' Mosby said. 'Rabbits is lucky. You'd better foller the luck an' go that way.'

"But Hunter was smart and didn't believe in signs. 'That's jest fool superstition,' he said. 'I like the looks of this crickbed to the right. You go ahead and foller that fool rabbit. I'll go to the right.'

"Well, he did go to the right, and right away he started pickin' up float and some nuggets. 'Way up the wash, where he picked up the last nugget, he hit on a ledge which showed gold. He located the Last Nugget right there, and come back chucklin' how he'd put it over on Mosby. Matter of fact, the Last Nugget did turn out to be a purty good ledge."

"And Mosby?" asked the interested Slade.

"Oh, Mosby. Well, Mosby follered his jack rabbit with the lucky hind foot . . . and located the Comstock!"

Farr drew a deep lungful of cigarette smoke and expelled it.

"Took Hunter quite a spell to get over that one," he added, "but he took it in sorta good part. For a long time, though, he spent lots of time prowlin' 'round in the hills and Dry Water Cañon tryin' to locate another Comstock, and never did.

"Then all of a sudden he give it up, started his Cattleman's Club about a year back, and has been doin' well at that. He's the sort what can't keep from meddlin' in things, though. Someday he'll burn his fingers proper."

"I noticed he had a bad burn on one of his fingers tonight," Slade remarked idly. "Looks sorta like he'd laid a cigarette against it, or touched a hot poker. By the way, does Hunter ever wear glasses?"

"Hell, no! That jigger's got shooting eyes. He can knock off a gnat's wing at twenty paces! Why?"

"Oh, I just wondered."

"Well, there's somethin' what's got me wonderin', and it's somethin' important. I'm wonderin' if that hellion is gonna show them other shells to Wyatt Cole. If he does, Wyatt's comin' hell-bent-for-election back here to look at the firin' pins of your guns, and your cake'll be dough. Hunter ain't got no use for me, and I reckon this is his way of takin' a smack at me."

Grinning slightly, Walt Slade drew his guns from their sheaths and emptied them. Gripping a leaden bullet between his white teeth, he wrenched it from the brass powder container. Then he shook his powder out on the floor. He did the same with a second cartridge.

Slipping the emptied shells into the guns, he cocked them and pulled the triggers. The caps exploded with sharp snaps, like striking matches. Slade ejected the shells into the palms of his hand.

"Hunter was jest a mite hasty in jumpin' at conclusions," he said softly. "He picked the wrong batch of shells in the alley. I figgered it wouldn't be a bad idea to let him fool himself a spell, and, anyway, I don't figger he's goin' to the sheriff, even when he sees I didn't scare outta town."

He held forth the cartridges for Farr to see. The firing pin mark on the cap of each was perfectly centered!

VII

"ROBBER'S ROOST"

Walt Slade rode to Harding, the railroad town, the following day. Guiding his tall black horse with his knees, he was playing his guitar and singing gaily. He passed the lumbering stage that bore the big gold shipment he had saved from the bank burglars the night before, although nobody but Carry Farr knew the truth of that business.

The outriders regarded him coldly as he swept past and stiffly answered his cheery greeting. A fleeting glance over his shoulder showed two of them with their heads together and the rest riding with added alertness. Slade chuckled and the guitar sang a lilting air.

In Harding he sent a long telegram that caused the operator, sworn to secrecy by the nature of his calling, to glance with startled attention at the tall man with the black hair and merry eyes.

"Oughta be an answer in a coupla days," Slade told him. "Hold it for me."

He got the answer two days later, an answer even more lengthy than the message he had dispatched. He was very thoughtful as he rode back to work at the Branding Pen.

Although he made no comment to Slade or anybody

else, Sliver Oakes thought it strange that every night when he had finished work, in the dead hours before dawn, his roomer should saddle the tall black horse and ride away into the darkness.

"Shadow needs exercise, and I do, too," Slade remarked the first night.

Sliver, who was good at attending to his own business, let it go at that.

Night after night he sat until the golden stars turned to silver and the sunlight glanced off the leaves and the prairie grasses burned purple and amethyst with a gemming of dew. Always he rode back to town by a roundabout way, avoiding the more traveled trails.

Then on one night of lashing rain and wailing wind he heard, welling from out the leaden east, that telltale drumming of swift hoofs. Tense, alert, he watched the horsemen, a dozen or more of them, sweep by in the graying shadows of the dawn. He noted, with a tightening of his firm mouth, that one of the two leaders of the troop rode with his right hand thrust into his shirt front.

He waited until the sound of hoofs had died away up the black cañon. Then he followed, knowing that the frowning walls of the narrow cañon would prevent his quarry from turning aside. Soon the rain had stopped, and it was light enough to make out the hoof marks of their passing. He could follow the trail with no difficulty.

Then, far up the cañon, the trail vanished where naked stone took the place of wet earth. There were some areas of impenetrable thicket. However, The Hawk did not worry. On either side the walls rose perpendicularly. A goat could not scale those walls, much less a troop of horsemen. He slowed the tall black as the concealing growth thinned and was intensely alert against possible ambush or against prematurely running into the mysterious horsemen.

For mile after mile the trail ran over the rocky floor, following at first what appeared to be the bed of an ancient river and then a mesa-like formation washed clean of soil by the rain water that rushed down its steep slope. It was past midday when The Hawk pulled his mount to a halt and sat staring with narrowed, coldly gray eyes, as the heavy sky crowded down onto the rim of the cañon.

The rocky floor had abruptly ended. Ahead was a wide expanse of stiff, wet clay into which a horse's hoof would sink almost to the fetlock. It extended from side wall to side wall and up the cañon as far as the eye could reach. Nowhere on its placid expanse could Slade see the mark of a passing hoof!

To make doubly sure he rode from side wall to side wall, eyeing every foot of the surface where the rock ended and the clay began. Reluctantly he admitted the indubitable truth.

"There just naturally hasn't been anybody riding this way since the rain stopped," he told the black horse. "And that means they didn't come this way!"

Shadow snorted cheerful agreement. Slade swore in exasperation.

"But where in hell did they go?" he demanded. "Those riders aren't flies or lizards, even though the chances are they're purty closely related to both. I tell you they just naturally *couldn't* have gone up the side walls anywhere!"

Shadow snorted again, and rolled a derisive eye. *Well, where in blazes did they go, then?* he seemed to ask.

"We'll find out," Slade told him grimly, "if I have to ride your legs down to your knees to do it."

Tediously, painstakingly, he began zigzagging back down the cañon, meticulously examining every foot of the towering side walls, peering into every thicket, riding around outcroppings of rock. Night came, and he hadn't even reached the beginning of the ancient riverbed.

"I reckon old Dot 'n' Carry'll be runnin' himself around in circles about now," he told Shadow as he removed the cayuse's trappings beside a trickle of clear water where a rich growth of grass promised the black horse a feast.

From staples he always carried in his saddlebags, he cooked a meal, with steaming coffee to wash it down. Then he smoked a cigarette, wished for his guitar, and went to sleep.

"They've got a hang-out somewhere in this damn' gully," he told Shadow the following morning. "Well, feller, we've nosed around in hole-in-the-wall country before now. We . . . say, mebbe that's *somethin'* . . . hole-in-the-wall! I wonder?"

With painstaking care he began his search again, but now he gave added attention to the bleak walls of the cañon. It was at the queer formation that looked like an ancient riverbed that he noticed something that narrowed his eyes and caused his pulses to beat faster.

For long minutes after pulling the cayuse to a halt, he sat and stared at a dense thicket that extended from the east wall of the cañon for nearly a hundred yards out onto the cañon floor. The ancient riverbed was choked with it at this point, and the trail up the cañon skirted the growth.

It was just a difference in coloration. At one point, instead of dusty-looking gray-green, the growth for several yards was slightly yellowish-brown in appearance. The Hawk's keen eyes probed the patch, and suddenly he whistled softly under his breath.

"The brush has been cut away there, shore as hell," he

muttered. "Cut away and then set back in place."

He spoke to the horse and diagonalled him across the cañon to where even denser growth ran along the west wall. As he had suspected, there was water beyond the growth and grass.

Shadow didn't take kindly to being forced through the thorny brush, but he made it without too much protest. Beside a deep pool formed by a tiny trickle from under the cañon wall, Slade took the gear off him and left him to crop the rich grass. He knew that the intelligent and well-trained animal would not leave the little clearing. Then he stealthily made his way back toward the east wall on foot.

The Hawk knew better than to remove the cut growth that had been cleverly put back into place. With the utmost care he wormed his way into the thicket at a little distance farther up the cañon.

Then he worked his way downcañon again. He was not at all surprised when at length he broke through a final fringe and found himself in a narrow lane, cut through the dense brush and worming toward the rock wall of the cañon. Nor was he unduly surprised when, on rounding a final turn of the lane, he saw a dark opening yawning in the cañon wall.

Slowly he glided forward, every sense alert, for the lane in the brush gave evidence of the recent passage of a number of horses. There were no signs of their presence at the moment, however, and The Hawk slipped on to the very lip of the opening. He paused, uncertain, and like an unexpected nightmare vision a man suddenly rose from behind a boulder.

The Hawk caught the flash of metal, weaved sideways, and clutched the descending knife hand with fingers like rods of nickel steel. A fist crashed against his jaw, and he went down, still clinging to a corded wrist, taking the man along with him.

Over and over they rolled amid the rocks, grimly silent, striking, wrenching, fighting with life as the stake. Slade still gripped the fellow's knife hand and lashed out with his other fist.

He had a quick glimpse of a dark, distorted face and blazing black eyes. Then the wrist was wrenched from his grip, and he hurled himself face downward in a split second of time. Over his prostrate body the thrown knife *buzzed* like an angry hornet.

Slade surged to his knees, hands flashing down. He saw the black muzzle of a gun yawning toward him, and then his own Colts roared deafeningly.

A bullet *whizzed* past The Hawk's ear as the dark man, already dead on his feet, pulled trigger with a last convulsive spasm of his muscles. Slade surged erect as the man fell, smoking guns jutting forward. Then he holstered the Colts and for a long moment stood listening.

But after the echoes of the triple report had ceased to slam about among the rocks, the silence remained unbroken. Waiting still longer, Slade dragged the body into the brush and carefully concealed it. Then cautiously he entered the dark opening.

It was so dark that almost immediately he retraced his steps to the thicket, constructed several torches of dry branches, and lighted one before entering the opening once more.

The smoky flame disclosed crowding walls of dark rock, scoured perfectly smooth by the action of water. Slade followed the comparatively narrow tunnel for a hundred yards or more and suddenly found himself in a wide room. The rock roof was so high above his head as to be invisible in the torchlight.

Holding the torch aloft, he sidled along the wall of the cave, noting where horses had recently been tethered to rings set in the stones. One horse was still there, probably belonging to the look-out. He moved on a little farther, and paused to stare at what was stacked in orderly rows. Bending down he prodded one of the stout buckskin sacks and found where the end was roughly sewn.

All ready to be loaded into an aparejo *on a mule's back,* he mused. *Sacks full of high-grade gold ore, or I'm a heap mistaken. This is getting interesting.*

Leaving the filled sacks, of which there were many, he continued to explore the cave. In the far wall was another opening of about the same width as that which led to the outer air. This apparently wound away into the bowels of the mountain east of the cañon wall.

Slade hesitated a moment, then strode on, questing forward with his torch. Soon he heard a low murmuring that, a little later, he identified as a considerable body of running water.

Louder and louder grew the sound until in the light of the torch he saw a curving lip of water that rushed down the far side of a vast gulf upon the edge of which he stood. As he gazed into the awful depths, Slade's scalp prickled. Up from the misty blackness came only the faintest of murmurings.

Hell, what a hole! he thought to himself. *Can't even hear the water hit bottom, and that's a pretty good-size creek running down this tunnel. Uhn-huh, this is where the water that used to run down the cañon, years and years ago, came from. That bottomless hole opened up, and the creek tumbled in there.*

He carefully skirted the gulf and found that there was ample room to walk along the rocky bank of the stream. He also saw signs of much passing back and forth. His feet crunched on bits of fallen ore. He saw cigarette butts and other things that denoted that men in considerable numbers had been using the tunnel over a period of time.

Slade had covered a distance that he estimated at considerably more than a mile when he came to a flight of rude steps leading upward into an opening that pierced the side wall of the tunnel. With even greater caution than before, he crept up the steps, which appeared to have been cut in the natural upward slope of a shallow side tunnel or room. A moment later and he was feeling along the surface of a wooden door.

Delicately balanced on oiled hinges, the door swung easily to the pressure of his hand. Slade found himself in another tunnel dark as the one he had just left. But this tunnel, he realized, was not a natural passage blown out by exploding gases of volcanic origin or hollowed by the continued action of water. This gallery was man-made. The roof was supported by heavy timbers, as were also the side walls, at regular intervals. The door through which he had come was, in fact, cunningly made to appear as part of the supporting timbering of the gallery.

As The Hawk stood uncertainly, there drifted to his ears the sound of a distant booming explosion. Listening intently, he could make out the sound of metal striking against rock.

This is one of the worked-out galleries of a mine, he quickly deduced. *And I'm plumb willing to bet something pretty it's John Mosby's Comstock. Looks like the mystery of the Comstock's missing high-grade ore isn't much of a mystery any more.*

For several minutes he stood in the gallery, undecided as to what use to make of his strangely acquired knowledge.

Then, a plan forming in his mind, he softly opened the door, glided down the damp stone steps, and hurried back along the winding tunnel of the cave.

He approached the opening to the cañon very cautiously, but the thicket was silent and deserted. A few minutes later, Shadow fled down the cañon like a frightened patch of animated midnight, leading the look-out's horse.

VIII

"END OF A CROOKED TRAIL"

Behind the locked doors of his office, old John Mosby listened with profane comment to what Carry Farr had to tell him.

"How the hell did you happen to hit onto this thing?" he demanded when Carry had finished the story in which he had been carefully coached by Walt Slade.

"Jest stumbled onto it plumb by accident," Carry replied. "I don't know who the gang is that's robbin' you . . . that's for you and the sheriff to find out . . . but I'll bet my last *peso* they'll be slippin' into the cañon for that ore tonight."

"You're shore that damn' hole in the ground runs into the Comstock?"

"What other mine could it run into?" countered Carry. "Is there any mine 'tween the Comstock and Dry Water Cañon? Doesn't your worked-out diggin's run west to mighty nigh the wall of the cañon?"

"Reckon that's so," admitted Old John. "Wait, I'll get the sheriff. . . ."

Nobody but John Mosby, the sheriff, and his trusted deputies knew of the posse that slipped out of Cholla long after dark that night. That is, nobody other than Carry Farr and Walt Slade, and Slade was not with the posse that Carry guided to the spot where the concealed lane was cut through the growth to the cave in the cañon wall.

Hidden in dense shadows, The Hawk sat his tall black horse at the edge of the thicket on the far side of the narrow cañon. Unseen, unheard, he watched the posse arrive and take up their stations on either side of the lane.

"We gotta get 'em with the goods," the sheriff had cautioned his men. "We gotta let 'em get inside, load their mule train, and start out. Then we'll throw down on 'em when they come through the brush. Have your flares all ready to light, you fellers, and toss 'em right up to the edge of the brush. Then we can see them, and even in the moonlight they won't get much of a glim at us.

"We gotta be on our toes, though. They're liable to get suspicious of somethin' not bein' jest right when they don't find the guard they left there, once they finished sneakin' high-grade outta the mine last night."

Wearily the hours passed for the tense watchers. The false dawn fled across the sky like a frightened ghost. The darkness seemed to intensify as a dull moon sank lower in the west. Then, suddenly, a faint *clicking* sounded. It grew to the muffled beat of hoofs.

A long line of shadowy shapes loomed out of the darkness of the lower cañon. They paused at the edge of the thicket. Men spoke in low gutturals. There was a noise of breaking brush as the lane was opened. One by one the ghostly shapes vanished into the growth.

Minutes passed; the unseen watchers gripped their weapons, made ready. A faint *clicking* sounded again, and a weirdly distorted form appeared to the accompaniment of rustling and crackling brush.

It was a mule bearing a huge *aparejo,* or pack sack. A mounted man followed it. Then came more loaded mules, and more horsemen. Finally the watchers could dimly see men shoving back into place the cut brush that hid the lane. Sheriff Wyatt Cole's bull bellow shattered the silence.

"Get your hands up! You're kivered, right and left. In the name of the State of Texas! You're under arrest!"

Almost instantly flares blazed up. They were tossed to the edge of the thicket, revealing a huddle of loaded mules and mounted men frozen in grotesque attitudes. The flickering flames also dimly showed the grim posse men, cocked rifles to their shoulders, eyes glinting back of the sights.

There was a crawling second of paralyzed inaction. Then from the huddled mob a gun blazed. A posse man went down with a queer little grunt. Instantly the leveled rifles flamed and roared. Men and mules fell like grain before a reaper's sickle.

There was a wild scattering, a spiteful *crackle* of six-guns. Crashing out from the milling group burst two horsemen. They sped down the cañon, posse bullets whining about them.

Instantly the watching Hawk went into action. He spoke to the black horse, and Shadow poured his long body over the ground.

One of the fleeing horsemen was falling behind his companion, who was superbly mounted. Shadow, fleeting through the pale moonlight and the paler light of the breaking dawn, swiftly overhauled him. The rider turned in his saddle, and flame gushed from his extended hand. The left, Slade noticed, as he threw down with his own guns.

Slade heard the bullet scream past his face, felt the wind of the second one. His Colts bucked in his hands, smoke wisping up.

The fleeing rider suddenly reeled in his saddle, leaned slowly sideways, and then fell. The riderless horse fled wildly to one side. Walt Slade, thundering past, leaned in his saddle and glanced into the dead face of Park Crony, the giant foreman of Howard Hunter's Last Nugget Mine.

Far ahead, the other ore thief was crashing toward the mouth of the cañon, leaning low in his saddle, urging a splendid bay horse on.

"Damn' lucky it's gettin' light," muttered Slade, settling himself in the hull. "If it was stayin' dark, he'd be mighty apt to give us the slip, and I've a plumb notion that's the big skookum he-wolf of the outfit himself." He added a little later: "Uhn-huh, I can see his black whiskers."

The bay showed wonderful speed, but steadily the tall black closed the distance. Soon he was within pistol range of the straining fugitive, but Slade held his fire. With unexpected suddenness the end came.

Like a shot rabbit, the big bay went end over end, hurling his rider from the saddle like a stone from a sling. Horse and man crashed through the brush, fell, and the man lay still.

"Put his foot in a badger hole, shore as hell!" exclaimed Slade as Shadow hurtled forward.

Almost before the tall black came to a plunging halt, Slade was out of the saddle. His feet touched the ground as the rider of the bay surged erect, hand flickering to his gun with a speed like the beat of a bird's wing. It was oily-smooth perfection, that draw, and blinding fast, but The Hawk's big Colt *boomed* a breath-second before smoke wisped from the black-bearded man's gun.

Slade felt the stinging burn of a bullet flicking the skin from his bronzed cheek. He stood sternly erect, holding his fire as the bearded man let his gun fall from a nerveless hand, and slowly sank to the ground.

An instant later, The Hawk was kneeling beside him, gazing into the already dimming blue eyes. With deft fingers he gripped the black beard, slipped the hooks that held it in place from over the man's ears, and revealed the distorted but still strangely beautiful face of Howard Hunter, owner of the Last Nugget Mine. Painfully, slowly, Hunter raised himself on a shaking elbow.

"Damn you," he gasped, "why couldn't you go back and look for some pickin's of your own! Why'd you have to horn into my game?"

Slade shook his black head. "Not horning in, Hunter," he replied softly, "just bustin' up your game. That's my business, busting up crooked games."

He held out his hand. Hunter, still wavering on his unsteady elbows, stared at a silver star set in a silver circle. With a gasp he sank back.

"A Ranger!" he panted. "A Texas Ranger! My God, El Halcón, a Ranger!"

"Yes, Slade of the Rangers. Undercover man with Captain McNelty's company."

A ghost of a smile flitted over the dying man's face. "And you're the troop Mosby asked to be sent over. Well, that's the Ranger way of doin' things. I was all ready to cut operations the minute the Rangers showed up. You fooled me proper. Trail's end, Ranger! End of a crooked trail. I was a mining engineer once . . . a good one. Got mixed up in crooked work. That's how I got next to handling burglar tools. Found that cave while prospecting in the cañon. Triangulated the route it took and the distance and figured it would be easy to get into the Comstock from it. Got an outfit of my old pals together, and that was the Dawn Riders. Pulled the robberies to get quick money for 'em.

Was aiming to get rich on the high-grade and go straight
. . . can't straighten a crooked trail, Ranger!"

He sank back, his blue eyes fixed and cold. Slade rocked
on his heels and rolled a cigarette. When Sheriff Cole rode
up, his eyes filled with suspicion, his gun hand ready, the
silver star of the Ranger was not in sight.

"I had to come along with my boss in case something
went wrong," Slade explained easily. "When those two
fellers bust loose, I figgered I'd ought to foller 'em."

"You did a good job . . . this time, anyway," the sheriff
grudgingly admitted. "But hereafter don't you be so damn'
ready with them guns. You ain't got no peace officer
'thority to back you up. If you'd made a mistake, you'd
have been in a mighty serious fix. My God, I never would
have believed this of Hunter!"

The posse rode back to town with their prisoners and the
bodies of the dead outlaws. Slade and Carry Farr dropped
some distance behind. Carry had some questions to ask.

"I first got a line on Hunter that day when they was
packin' Last Nugget ingots into the bank," Slade told him.
"Those ingots were two kinds of gold . . . yellow and red. I
never heard tell of one mine producing both kinds. Then
when I saw a Comstock ingot and it was red gold, I got to
thinkin' in terms of Hunter and his mine.

"Then that night of the bank burglary, Hunter slipped
bad. Of course, he knew he couldn't do anything with the
stage next day, the way it was guarded, so he took a long
chance and tried to crack the vault.

"If I hadn't played a hunch that night, he would have got
away with it. One of the jiggers there that night had black
whiskers, like the boss of the Dawn Riders was said to have.
When Hunter came to the saloon, I saw marks on his ears
like what are made by the side frames of glasses. The hooks

that hold false whiskers on make those kind of marks, too, and you said Hunter didn't wear glasses. And on his finger was a fresh burn, the kind a drill bit will make when it gets hot from boring through steel.

"Next day I telegraphed headquarters at Franklin to try and get a line on Hunter's past. That wasn't hard, and they found he'd done time back East for burglary and other things. I figgered that Hunter was in some way gettin' high-grade from the Comstock and stampin' it in his own mill. I took to layin' for the Dawn Riders, got a line on them as they passed along the Cholla Trail . . . and the rest was easy."

"Uhn-huh, easy as turnin' a mountain over with a tooth-pick! It's a damn' shame, feller, that you don't never get no credit for what you do. To 'most everybody you're jest The Hawk, a ridin' *hombre* what some queer stories are told 'bout and who sheriffs figger will bear watchin'!"

Farr's face flushed with indignation, but Slade, thinking of the smile and the handclasp of stern old Captain McNelty, Grand Old Man of the Rangers, was content.

Sheriff Cole grunted his relief when he heard that night that Walt Slade had given up his job at the Branding Pen and left Cholla.

"You never can tell 'bout them damn' wanderin' gun-slingers," declared the sheriff. "They ain't ever tied to anythin' steady and respectable, and they're liable to go owlhoot 'most any time."

But Walt Slade sang gaily as he rode through the pale starlight, playing his little guitar and joking with his black horse. In his pocket was a message from Captain McNelty, a message that sent the undercover man on a mission that promised excitement and danger. The Hawk was on the trail again, and happy.

TERROR STALKS THE BORDER

I

"OUT OF THE STORM"

Starred with silver and banked in jet, the stately River of the Palms rolled toward the distant blue waters of the Gulf. In the shadow of majestic mountains, through the wind-rippled grasses of the rangeland, past the grating, whispering sands of the desert, the tawny flood swept onward, tireless, irresistible, eternal.

When time and the world were young, it was born amid the crash and thunder of rising mountains. Once the desert through which it now flowed was a shallow sea swarming with strange and ferocious life. The inexorable hand of the ages brushed away the brackish waters of the gray, turbulent sea.

The fierce sun of earth's lusty youth dried the reeking sands. The lonely winds that walked the desolate world lifted and shifted the sands, used them as hammer and chisel to carve the stranded islands into weird and grotesque buttes. The monstrous life forms passed away. The mountains grew tall, their cone summits giving place to spire and fang, dizzy crags that raked the brassy heavens and were shaped by the fingers of the rain, the wind, and the frost. Only the old river remained the same, rolling onward to a more distant sea.

Under the hot blaze of the Southwest Texas stars, the

muddy flood churned its way between desolate stretches of desert. Here, instead of level or rolling plains mantled with grass, were battlement and mesa, fault and escarpment, strange forms of tower and chimney and grotesquely carved butte. Here grew the cactus in myriad species, the greasewood, and the sage. Here the Mexicans of the dreamy land of *mañana* south of the river and "Mexicans" of the north tilled their scanty crops, their lives bound to and by the river.

It held together rather than separated the Mexicans of old Mexico and the American citizens of pure Mexican blood who, with their ancestors several times removed, were born and reared on Texas soil. All depended on the yellow stream to save them from the desert and to make their mutual poverty and distress at least bearable. The river villages depended for their very existence upon the Río Grande.

Doreto, the *peón,* crouched beside the window of his adobe hut and stared into the night. From the hut's site, a little swell of land, he could see the shifting star shine of the river, could hear its monotonous sob and murmur. The smell of the hurrying flood waters was wafted to him on the wings of a lonesome little wind that wandered around the thatched adobe for a moment, before tramping on its weary way across the desert toward the grim battlements of the Huecos and Cerro Diablo. That wind, slanting wearily out of the southwest, was a silent wind save for the endless plaint of the river.

Doreto strained his ears to catch a sound he feared and dreaded, and expected. Abruptly his scrawny form stiffened and a murmured—*"Madre de Dios."*—slipped past his suddenly dry lips. The hurrying fingers of the wind had plucked up a sound other than that of the tireless river.

Faint it was, a silver-shod tapping sifting tremulously through the starlight, but it brought the sweat out on the *peón*'s thin cheeks and widened his dark eyes.

He crouched still lower beside the window, peering frantically into the shadows, the palms of his hands moist and sticky. On came the sound, a swelling beat that grew and grew. The quick, staccato drum of a fleet horse's hoofs rapped on the hard soil of the riverbank. It came, Doreto knew, from the direction of the ford across the Río Grande.

Up the little knoll, zigzagging along the trail worn deeply by many passages of bare feet, came the horseman, looming gigantically in the dim light. There was a final clash of hoofs, a breathless pause, then the crash of a heavy quirt handle against the closed door. With trembling hands the *peón* unbarred it, swung it open, and stood, head humbly bowed.

The horseman leaned forward in his saddle, hissed words in a harsh voice, peremptory words that brooked no argument.

Doreto's thin shoulders quivered submissively. "*Sí,*" he mumbled in thick acquiescence. "I come."

The horseman wheeled his mount, drummed down the tortuous trail, and vanished into the shadows, the fading *tip-tap* of swift hoofs shattering the silence for a numb moment or two and then dying into nothingness. Doreto turned to face his wife, who was staring at him with wide, tearful eyes from the gloom.

"You will not go, Doreto?"

"Not go! *¡Sangre de Cristo!* Not go when the Rider brings the summons! Think you of Miguel of the Ford, who did not go . . . crucified to the spines of a cholla cactus! Of Sebastian . . . bound to an ant hill, with the sun of noon pouring down into eyes from which the lids had been cut away! I fear to go, *si!* But I fear more to remain!"

Still muttering, Doreto fumbled among the cords of his bed and drew from beneath the husk mattress a long-barreled rifle. A moment later he vanished through the black opening of the door, in his ears the terrified sobbing of his wife.

Down the hill he hurried, turned west along the riverbank, and stumbled on through the gloom. As he went, a wall of inky clouds climbed up the long slant of the western sky, blotting out the stars and pressing a blanket of shadows down upon the ghostly gray surface of the river.

Overhead thunder muttered. There was an occasional flicker of lightning. Then, on the wings of a moaning wind, came the rain, level lances of icy water that beat and lashed the thin figure, staggering on in the glare of the lightning. The thunder's muttering grew to a crashing roar.

Through the desolation of wind and rain rode a man—a tall man mounted on a magnificent golden sorrel whose sleek coat streamed with water. The man cursed the rain in a half-humorous, half-weary voice, while the sorrel snorted his unqualified disgust.

"Feller, we may be goin' some place, but we shore ain't gettin' there, not so you can notice," the man said, blinking the water from his level green eyes.

The cayuse said something in horse language that obviously would not bear repeating. The man chuckled, his strongly molded, slightly wide mouth quirking up at the corners and his green eyes sunny.

The rider swayed in the saddle with the lithe grace of one who has spent a lifetime there. His broad shoulders shrugged under his streaming slicker whose clumsy folds could not altogether conceal the lines of deep chest, slim waist, and muscular thighs. His hair, what showed beneath the brim of his wide hat, was black as the storm clouds overhead and seemed to shed the rain without gathering any dampness. Still chuckling to himself, he rode westward into the teeth of the storm.

Out of the darkness ahead came a staccato tapping that swiftly grew to a drumming *thud.* The man on the sorrel straightened, his eyes questioning.

"Somebody shore seems t' be in a hurry," he murmured. "Mebbe he's scairt he'll get wet. Calculate we'd better give him room to pass."

He reined the big horse out of the trail and nearer the sloping bank of the river. Slouching comfortably in the saddle, he waited while the *thud* of the swift hoofs grew louder and louder.

In a blaze of golden flame the "roses of the storm" suddenly bloomed across the heavens, making the streaming landscape as bright as day. The man on the sorrel had a quick vision of a dark, twisted face rushing toward him out of the night, that and the lightning flicker of a sinewy hand.

Crash! Crash! Crash!

The tall man was sidewise out of the saddle before death blazed at him out of the dark. He heard the bullets yell through the space his body had occupied the instant before. Only his astounding co-ordination of mind and muscle had saved him.

As he left the saddle, his right hand closed on the butt of the heavy rifle snugged in the saddle boot. In that one, bewildering ripple of lithe movement he whirled on firm feet and flung the rifle to his shoulder. Long lances of flame spurted as he raked the darkness ahead with lead. He paused for an instant, finger curled on the trigger. Out of the dark came the retreating drum of the racing horse. Again he fired, three swift shots, center, right, and left.

The lightning flared again, revealing a speeding figure bending low over the neck of a horse. The tall man's eyes glinted back of the rifle sights, but even as he pressed the trigger again, man and horse lurched sideward into the solid blackness of a grove that grew beside the trail. The darkness rushed down as the lightning died. The roll of the thunder drowned all other sounds.

The tall man hesitated a second, then fumbled cartridges from his saddlebags and reloaded the rifle.

"Ain't no sense in chasin' after that galoot," he told the sorrel. "Chances are, Goldy hoss, you could run him down, all right, if we managed to hit onto his trail, but chances are, too, that we'd have to hunt half the night before we picked it up.

"Funny thing to do, throw down on a perfect stranger thataway. Looks sorta like he's got somethin' on his mind. Mebbe we jest scairt him, though. 'Pears folks get scairt sorta easy in this section, accordin' to what we heard about it. Ain't much wonder, though, when you recollect what all's happened over thisaway of late.

"Well, everything considered, I guess little Jim Hatfield and his Goldy hoss had best be amblin' along toward where that there town of Cuevas and *Don* Fernando Cartina's F Bar C Ranch is supposed to be. June along, you jughead, it's a hungry night, and sorta dampish!"

II

"DEATH'S SHADOW"

The storm brawled on across the sky, and in its wake a wind scoured the sky clean with final wisps of cloud. The stars, newly rinsed and burnished, blazed out again, but only for a little while. Soon they paled from gold to silver, grew white and wan, shrank to mere pinpoints of light, and then winked out.

As the retreating storm vanished beyond the eastern horizon, the sky flushed delicate rose, deepened to soft pink barred with gold. Bands of scarlet climbed up from the edge of the world, merged in a bewildering crimson flame shot with saffron arrows.

The desert shimmered like polished bronze. The western mountains veiled themselves in exquisite purple. A bird sang. The grasses rippled blue and indigo. The sun came forth like a bridegroom from his chamber, and it was day.

Jim Hatfield, Texas Ranger, rode through the winey gold of morning as he had ridden through the rain-lashed blackness of the night. The sun quickly dried his sodden clothes and the glossy coat of the big sorrel. Beside a brook of clear water he dismounted, turned the horse loose to graze, and cooked his breakfast with swift efficiency.

Hot coffee, bacon, dough cake fried in the grease—he downed them all with the lusty appetite of youth and perfect health. Then, while the golden horse still cropped, he stretched out in the shade of a thicket and slept like a child. Two hours later he sat up, thoroughly awake, grinned at the sun, and got lithely to his feet.

The stream formed a shady pool beside the thicket, and Jim stripped and plunged in, sousing his long, lean body in the refreshing water. As he moved, the muscles rippled along sinewy back and shoulders under a skin that had the sheen of satin. Flexing his long arms, he stepped from the pool, and stopped dead still.

Three men had ridden up, the slight sound of their horses' unshod hoofs on the grass-grown bank covered by the prattle of the stream. Silent, motionless, they sat and stared at the tall Ranger.

Double cartridge belts crossed their chests. They carried rifles. A heavy revolver and a long knife sagged at the waist belt of each. They were dark of face, beady of eye, with high cheek bones and lank black hair. Almost pure-blood Yaqui Indians, Jim noticed instantly.

"Buenas días," nodded the Ranger, his voice mild and drawling. Silence greeted his "Good day." The beady eyes remained inscrutable. Jim swept the dark faces with his level green gaze, apparently only mildly interested, but thinking furiously.

He was totally unarmed, his gun belt being half a dozen yards distant. The sinister trio had noted the fact, as he gathered from the quick, furtive glances they cast in the direction of his discarded garments. To all appearances, he was utterly at their mercy, and it did not need a second glance to tell him that these were men to whom the very meaning of the word was unknown.

"What do you here, *señor?*" asked one, his voice the harsh growl of a beast of prey.

"Right now," Hatfield told him, "I am taking a bath. I'm jest passin' through."

The other's face did not change. "We want no *gringos* here," he said with cold finality.

"I ain't stayin'," the Ranger replied.

The Mexican's upper lip lifted in what was intended for a smile, showing sharply pointed white teeth—a smile of sinister menace. *"Señor,"* he said softly, "you make the mistake. You *are* staying here!"

At the words his companions slightly shifted their rifles, and a dark glitter, like the glint of bloody dagger points in the sun, birthed in their beady eyes.

The meaning of both words and gesture was unmistakable. Jim Hatfield realized it and knew he was in a desperate position. It was not the first time that the Lone Wolf had found himself facing desperate odds. In the course of his career as a Ranger, death had many more times than once missed him by the thickness of a shadow on a gray day. Some of his fellow Rangers vowed that he possessed a charmed life.

What Jim Hatfield *did* possess were nerves and muscles that obeyed instantly and without fumbling the swift orders of a hair-trigger mind. Working alone, as was his custom, he could seldom look for assistance. His facile mind, his steely muscles, and lightning-fast hands were what he depended upon. In addition to these, however, there was one friend, usually within call, upon whom he could depend to the utmost of the friend's limited capabilities. He could see that friend now, lifting an inquiring golden head over a clump of bush. He saw, also, the ripple of muscle along the Mexican leader's jaw as he made up his mind to act, that and the tensing of the dark hands that held the rifle.

Still standing unclothed and unarmed, the Ranger threw back his head and pursed his lips. A whistle note, shrill and piercing, thrilled through the sultry air. Swift on its heels came the Lone Wolf's deep-toned shout.

"Get 'em, Goldy hoss! At 'em, boy!"

Instantly there was a prodigious crashing of shod hoofs and a scream of rage. Down upon the startled Mexicans stormed the great golden horse, pawing, slashing, biting. One of the wiry little mustangs was bowled over like a rabbit, his rider with him. A second man shrieked in agony as the sorrel's gleaming teeth tore a great piece of flesh from his arm.

They tried to shoot the tall horse, but his movements were so lightning fast and his attack so vicious they could not draw a bead on him. And in a split second of time they had other things to think about.

Jim Hatfield covered the distance to his gun belt like a bronze streak in the sunshine. As he yanked the heavy Colts from their sheaths, the dark-browed leader of the Mexicans sent a rifle bullet screaming over his shoulder. A second clipped a lock of dark hair from his head. Then his guns let go with a rippling crash.

The dark leader died in his saddle, with two bullets laced through his heart. As he toppled to the ground, Hatfield shot the unhorsed man between the eyes as the man tried to pull trigger. He flung up his guns as the third man, blood pouring from his slashed arm, went crashing through the growth on his maddened horse.

By the time Hatfield got around the thicket, he was out of range, slumped low in his saddle, apparently in a faint. The Ranger watched him until he was small in the distance, still reeling drunkenly but clinging to his flying mustang. Hatfield shrugged, and went back for his clothes.

"Calculate he won't be good for much of anythin' except to yowl for quite a spell," he growled. "Well, yaller hoss, you shore did yourself proud. I'll remember the next time you try to kick me loose from my pants or bite my ear off. Yeah, you're quite a cayuse, even if you are so pizen-mean a rattlesnake'd swell up and bust if he fanged you."

He rubbed the velvety muzzle affectionately and ducked as the broncho reached for his ear. He whirled, guns stabbing out, as a voice spoke from the growth behind him.

"*¡Madre de Dios! Señor,* you are not long for this world!"

Over the muzzles of his ready guns, Jim eyed the speaker, a wizened old Mexican who was staring fearfully at the sprawled bodies on the grass. He raised frightened eyes to the half-clothed Ranger and shook his grizzled head.

"Two dead," he mumbled thickly. "Two riders! And one who escaped to tell the tale!"

"Tell it to whom, *amigo?*" Hatfield asked, putting up his guns and smiling at the old *peón.*

The other wet his dry lips with a quivering tongue. "Assuredly," he mumbled, "assuredly will he tell El Hombre."

"The Man?" Hatfield translated wonderingly. "What man?"

"El Hombre is El Hombre," replied the *peón.* "None may say more than that. None may *know* more than that."

"You gonna tell him, too?" Jim Hatfield asked quietly.

The other let out a choked-chicken squawk, and his few teeth chattered. "*Señor,*" he gasped, "I saw nothing. I but rested here in the shade. I know nothing. I speak to El Hombre? God forbid, that I should speak to him or that he speak to me."

His fear-contorted face vanished, and Hatfield heard him running swiftly through the growth. The Ranger finished his dressing thoughtfully, the concentration furrow creased deeply between his level black brows.

"Funny business," he mused. "Riders and El Hombre. Mexicans usually mean a lot more than jest The Man when they use words like that. About like when we say the big boss. Hmm. So El Hombre has jiggers ridin' for him that don't want *gringos* around here. Evidently The Man doesn't want 'em . . . the riders were jest following orders. That hard-ridin' gent I met last night in the rain felt that way, too, evidently. Things sorta tie up all the way.

"And it all ties with what Captain Bill McDowell told me about the trouble over thisaway. Those three hellions . . . the one last night, too . . . look like the sort of hydrophobic skunks that would peg poor devils over ant hills and cut off their eyelids, or hang 'em up on cholla cactuses.

"I would 'a' held that ol' jigger that jest scooted off and found out if he knew anythin', only he was too scairt to be of any use. I know the kind . . . scare 'em and all they do is lie a blue streak. Well, hoss, reckon the best thing is to keep right on junin' along till we hit Cuevas or *Don* Fernando Cartina's spread. I calculate that's our best bet to get the lowdown on things."

A careful search of the dead men's clothing revealed nothing that shed any light on the mystery, so Jim Hatfield saddled Goldy and rode west once more. Overhead, outlined against the clear blue of the sky, an ominous shape sailed slowly on planing wings. Another joined it, and another. Lower they glided and low, wrinkled, featherless necks outstretched, beady, dispassionate eyes staring coldly—death's winged ambassadors. For the briefest flicker of an instant, the dark shadow of one rested on the Ranger's face.

III

"HOT LEAD"

"There's some kinda merry blue-blazin' hell busted loose over in the Cuevas Valley country, Jim," grim old Captain Bill McDowell, commander of the "Last Frontier" post of the Rangers at Franklin, had told Jim Hatfield one afternoon after perusing a scrawled letter and a second missive inscribed in a singularly neat and legible hand. He glanced up at his ace man and frowned back at the letters.

"Here's a yowl from Sheriff Raines of Cuevas County," he went on. "Raines writes that the whole district appears to have gone loco . . . everybody is scairt bald-haided and with plenty of reason. Not jest ord'nary killin's and things, but the sorta dados the Comanches and Apaches usta kick up 'fore we tamed 'em down a bit.

"Sez there's a dozen poor devils been tortured on cactus and ant hills. The big ranches have lost a passel of steers. Been a few stagecoach robberies and a raid on the Cuevas bank, which didn't have no luck.

"Appears old Ab Carlyle, the president, who usta fight with Houston, was settin' in his office with a sawed-off shotgun and a coupla sixes handy when the larceny-minded gents rode up. Ab accounted for two of the sidewinders, and t'other three got away."

He paused a moment, and his lined face grew blank. "I knowed old Ab," he said softly. "Worked with him as a hand on Slaughter's Rockin' Chair spread."

Jim had glanced inquiringly at his chief.

"They found Ab in a alley two days later," Cap'n Bill

went on. "Throat was cut from ear to ear, and other things done to him, Raines writes. He didn't say jest what . . . must've been purty bad."

Hatfield said nothing, but his own strangely colored eyes turned the shade of snow-dusted ice on a bitter winter morning.

Captain Bill nodded, understanding perfectly. "There's more," he added, "but we'll let that pass for right now. Raines is bawlin' for a troop of Rangers to clean up the district. There's another letter here from *Don* Fernando Cartina, biggest rancher out that way, owns the F Bar C spread and has a interest in the mines around Cuevas, and such.

"They evidently wrote 'em together in Raines's office. *Don* Fernando substantiates what Raines says and figgers, too, a troop is needed. Calculate the *don* doesn't know any better, but Raines oughta. He should know that with the Comanche trouble up nawth and them rows over to the salt flats we ain't got no troop to spare right now."

"Raines is a real old-timer, ain't he?" remarked Hatfield.

"Uhn-huh, and from what I know of him, things must really be purty bad over there, for, as I remember, Jed Raines is a salty proposition."

"Does he say anything about who he calculates is responsible for the hell-raising?"

"Oh, Jed blames the Mexicans fust thing off, which is nacheral with him. He had plenty trouble with 'em in the old days and figgers they ain't none of 'em any good. Things is sorta peculiar over there, you know . . . four, five thousand Mexicans live in the county, that is they're Mexican blood . . . they're Texas born and American citizens, but fellers like Jed Raines calls 'em Mexicans.

"Then there's about seven thousand livin' in the villages

jest t'other side of the river. Of course, they visit back and forward and mingle and have their feasts t'gether and intermarry and what not. Hard to tell where the Mexican leaves off and the Texan begins with them folks.

"Funny thing about the business we're considerin', though, and somethin' Jed didn't seem to get hep to a-tall is that most of the people what hev been killed and tortured is Mexicans. Seems if the Mexicans really was back of it all, they'd go sorta easy on their own kind."

Hatfield nodded agreement to this, and the captain continued: "So, seein' as we shore ain't got no troop to hustle there and mop things up, I calculate you'd better mosey over and find out what's goin' on. Sergeant Aiken can take charge of the boys over to the salt flats, instead of you, as I'd figgered fust. If you need help, you can let out a squawk, and I'll see what I can do for you."

"Yeah, I'll do that," agreed the Lone Wolf as he got to his feet, took the two letters for a more thorough study of their contents, and left the room.

"Uhn-huh, like hell you will," chuckled Captain Bill as the door closed on the Ranger's broad back. "When *you* yell for help, me, I'm gonna fork me the fastest hoss what's handy and hightail . . . in t'other direction, 'cause right then I calculate the only person what can do anybody any good is the Almighty Hisself."

It had been said about Hatfield that he would charge hell with a bucket of water, and it carried considerable weight among the Rangers.

Hatfield was going over in his mind the contents of those two letters as he rode into the red eye of the sunset. He had destroyed the missives themselves, but his photographic memory retained their minutest details. Right now he was checking the directions they gave for reaching Cuevas.

"Calculate that sawtooth mountain ahead is the one that Raines said was right back of the town," he mused aloud, squinting at the lofty peak about whose massive shoulders the approaching dusk was drawing a robe of royal purple. "Letter said Cuevas was built at the foot of a spur that runs down almost to the river. Guess the hills that sorta make easy stepping up to the mountain is where the mines are. Mighty fine-lookin' rangeland between here and those hills. Funny thing, stretch of range like this set down almost in the middle of the desert. This whole section is what's left of a high plain that was worn down more by wind and sun beating on a bare surface than by rain. Now we big-feeling jiggers come crawlin' around the foot of them old spires that have been lookin' down on things hereabouts for more millions of years than even the geologists can agree on. Guess we ain't such a much after all, Goldy hoss."

He smiled reminiscently, recalling windy arguments he had heard between certain eminent geologists. Hatfield had studied mining engineering, in which geology had naturally played a large part. After his father's death, Hatfield had been thrown on his own resources, and he had instinctively turned to ranching and had worked as a cowboy on a number of spreads. Cowboy, prospector, rider of the dim trails—two countries and a dozen states and territories had known him before, drifting back to Texas, he had joined the Rangers. Now he was Lieutenant under Roaring Bill McDowell and stationed in the dark and bloody southwest corner of Texas, a section larger than many Eastern states, sparsely settled, grim, forbidding.

"No law west of the Pecos," men had said for years. Jim Hatfield and his intrepid companions of the "Frontier Legion" had brought law to the district—Ranger law—but administering it was a hard and dangerous task and a never-ending one.

Jim Hatfield's standing with the Rangers was a unique one. Taciturn old Lieutenant Carney had defined it perfectly when Hatfield first came west to join McDowell's troop. "When he's with a troop, he's jest another good Ranger," said Carney, "but when he's off alone, he's a holy terror. Ain't never failed to outfight and outsmart any smooth, salty *hombre* that's went up against him. He's a lone wolf, that's what he is."

The name had stuck, and the Lone Wolf had time and again justified Carney's statement. He was Roaring Bill McDowell's trouble-shooter, the rock-faced captain's last answer to the lawless element of his grim and desolate district.

The sun sank lower. The light rays leveled out and tinged the blue wind-ripples of the prairie grass with flame. Hatfield could make out a faint smudge rising against the blaze of the western sky. He knew it to be the smoke from the smelters and stamp mills of Cuevas, the raw, turbulent gold-strike town clinging to the gray flanks of the hills.

"Got another hour or so of daylight," he calculated, squinting at the low-lying sun. "Hoss, I figger we might as well eat before trying to make it into town. Things look closer in this air than they really are . . . quite a step over to that ridge. As for you, you ol' grass burner, all you gotta do is drop your nose down and help yourself to a square meal any time you take a notion. Get goin', you jughead, we'll point for that creek over to the left. Right now my stomach's so empty she's slid clean in behind my backbone."

The creek, a shallow trickle of clear water with sedgy banks, was lined with a moderately wide belt of thick growth. Hatfield headed for a little clearing that opened out onto the prairie across which he was riding. On the far side of the stream, the clearing was walled in by thick bristles of chaparral. It sloped gently to the water's edge.

The sorrel was thirsty. "All right," Hatfield told him, "you go ahead and drink while I get a fire started. Then I'll slip the rig off you, and you can take a roll. We aren't staying here long."

With the efficiency of an old campaigner, the Ranger had a clear blaze going in a very few minutes. He carefully stacked more dry wood on it, desiring a bed of glowing coals over which cooking could be done with a minimum of smoke and resulting profanity. He was turning to care for the horse when a muffled, querulous bawl sounded a little distance down the stream.

Hatfield glanced that way, noted the deeper green of swampland, and listened for a repetition of the bawl. It came again, undoubtedly from a weary and struggling throat. Hatfield had heard that kind of a bellow before, times without number. Instead of uncinching the sorrel, he swung into the saddle and loosened his rope.

"Damn' calf got himself bogged down in the mud," he remarked to Goldy. "C'mon, feller, we gotta snake him out."

The Ranger skirted a clump of growth, shoved the sorrel through another, and saw the calf. The animal, almost half grown, was firmly held in the sticky swamp mud. Already it had sunk to its knees. Soon it would be completely engulfed.

Hatfield measured the distance with his eye and flipped a lazy loop toward the straining head. The noose settled about the calf's neck, and the Ranger tightened it with an easy pull, so as not to strangle the dogie. Then he sent Goldy slowly up the bank, dragging the choking, squawking creature out of the mud.

Once the calf was in the clear, Hatfield eased off the pressure, and the calf floundered up the bank. It limped badly, however, and Hatfield could see a smear of blood on one haunch.

"Guess we'd better haul you over to the fire and take a look at that leg," he decided.

The calf didn't particularly want to go, but didn't have much choice in the matter. In the clearing, a quick flip of the rope and the creature went down. Hatfield dismounted, leaving Goldy to keep the rope taut, and bent over the calf, which lay bawling beside the fire.

"Not broke." He nodded, feeling of the injured limb. "Jest a bad cut. A little liniment on it, and you'll be OK." He straightened up to get the bottle from his saddlebags.

Wham!

Jim Hatfield turned a backward flip-flop as a bullet knocked his fire to smoking fragments. He felt the wind of it and felt a little more than the wind of a second shot that followed closely on its heels. That one knocked a bit of skin from the back of his left hand.

Before the third one got there, which it did without delay, he was hidden in the growth, swearing softly to himself and peering across the stream. A fourth slug showered him with leaves and twigs, but by that fourth shot he had located the approximate position of the gunman.

Silently as a wraith of drifting smoke, he faded through the growth, working swiftly upstream, where the creek was narrow and rock-strewn. He slipped around a bend and flitted across the stream, using the rocks for steppingstones. In the growth on the far bank he redoubled his caution as he glided back downstream.

The Ranger traveled away from the water until he was directly opposite the clearing. Moving with the smooth grace of a hunting lion, he approached the final fringe of thicket.

IV

"THE LION STRIKES"

Bill McDowell had once envisioned Jim Hatfield as a mountain lion poised on a lonely crag in the moonlight, ready to dare the black depths beneath in one tremendous, death-defying leap. Could the old Ranger captain have seen him at the moment, he would have been more than ever struck by the aptness of his simile.

The Lone Wolf's long, lithe body was crouched tensely, ready, muscles crawling along back and legs like powerful snakes. He had sensed rather than seen the slightest hint of movement at the base of a bush-shadowed boulder a little way down the sloping bank.

An instant later he leaped as the panther leaps, steely fingers outstretched. He landed beside the more solid shadow huddled behind the boulder and peering across the stream.

"Gotcha!" he growled exultantly. In another instant his arms were filled with a wildcat's fighting fury. He gave a gasp of amazement and tightened his grasp on the slim figure of a tiny, red-haired girl whose big blue eyes blazed into his and whose breath came between parted red lips.

Before he knew it, there was a long scratch down his left cheek and a couple more on his neck. White little teeth fastened on the back of his hand. A sun-golden little fist beat a tattoo on his broad chest.

"Hold it, miss!" he bawled. "I ain't gonna hurt you. I'll turn you loose if you promise to be good!"

For answer she kicked his shins with small riding boots and tried to bite a second time. Hatfield shook her till her teeth rattled and she gasped for breath.

"Listen, you little hellion!" he grated, "if you don't behave, I'm gonna turn you over my knee and spank you till you'll eat standin' up for a week! What's the matter with you, anyhow? You plumb loco?"

Suddenly he felt the little body go limp in his grasp. An instant later she broke into convulsive sobbing.

"I . . . I know you're going to kill me!" she gasped.

With effortless ease, Jim Hatfield picked her up, took her fallen rifle from beside the boulder with one hand, and strode with her out into the open. There he set her on her feet and regarded her in the last light of the dying day.

His green eyes were sunny, and his wide mouth was grinquirked at the corners. The girl stared at him, fear struggling with surprise. As he continued to smile down at her from his great height, the fear vanished altogether, and the surprise deepened.

"Why . . . why you can't be working for the Preston outfit!" she exclaimed.

"Preston outfit?" Hatfield repeated questioningly.

"Yes," said the girl, "Brant Preston's Circle P."

"Nope, I don't work for the Circle P," Hatfield told her. "What made you think I did?"

"Because," replied the girl angrily, "Brant Preston hires all the gunmen and rustlers that drift in here."

Her blue eyes flashed as she glanced across the stream where Goldy, obedient to orders, still held the rope taut on the protesting dogie.

"Even if you don't work for Brant Preston, I'd like to have you explain about altering the brand on my calf!" she demanded.

"Alterin' the brand on your calf?" Hatfield wondered. "Why, miss, I wasn't doin' no job of loose ironin'."

"What were you dragging it up to your fire for then?" she demanded. "I watched you throw and hog-tie it. Why did you do that if you weren't going to blot the brand?"

Hatfield chuckled, his green eyes sunnier than ever. "C'mon, *señorita*," he said, leading the way toward where he had crossed the stream, "the best thing I can do is show you what I was doin'. That'll explain things better'n talkin' about it."

When they reached the rocky narrows, Hatfield picked up the girl lightly and carried her across. She offered no objection, not even when he continued to carry her until they reached the clearing. The hog-tied calf gave a final weary and querulous bawl as they approached.

Hatfield gestured to its gashed haunch and to the mud with which it was smeared. As the girl examined the injured animal with little exclamations of pity, he procured the liniment bottle from his saddlebags and gave the wound a liberal application. The calf bellowed to high heaven as the fiery medicine soaked into the open wound, but, when the Ranger eased off the rope, it scrambled to its feet and limped off with many an indignant backward glance.

"He'll make out now," chuckled the Ranger. "Sore as hell, inside and out, but nothin' he won't get over."

He replaced the liniment bottle and slipped the rig off Goldy.

"Got time to eat with me?" he asked, hauling forth the makings of a meal. "I wanna make it to town tonight," he added, "and I figured there wasn't any sense in taking that ride on a empty stomach."

The girl hesitated. "I really should be heading back to the ranch," she said, "but I guess things can get along without me for a while."

She paused, and looked the tall Ranger full in the eyes.

"First thing, I wish to apologize for misjudging you," she said. "We have lost so much stock of late, that I was furious when I saw what appeared to be another theft going on right before my eyes. I'm sorry I knocked dust in your eyes."

"You came darn' near doin' more than knock it in my eyes. If you could jest shoot a bit straighter, you'd have dusted both sides of my coat."

The girl glanced at him, a ghost of a smile touching her red lips. She picked up the light rifle, and her eyes traveled over the clearing.

To the west, across the stream and quite a distance away, was a tall, blasted pine. On the topmost dead branch, an almost vertical spire of rotting wood, perched a hoary-headed old hawk, his gray shape outlined sharply against the fading red of the evening sky. Shadows were already clustering thickly in the clearing, and the light was dim and uncertain.

"Watch the hawk," she said, lifting the rifle.

"Hold on!" exclaimed Jim Hatfield. "Not that feller . . . those gray-legs are good citizens . . . don't eat anything but bugs and such."

"Oh, I won't hurt him," she replied, steadying the rifle. "Watch me knock his perch out from under him."

The next instant the amazed hawk was hurtling upward, squawking his indignation. The rotten branch on which he had roosted was spattering down through the tree and the echoes of the waspish rifle *crack* were blundering about among the trunks.

Jim Hatfield nodded gravely to the smiling girl. "Thank you, miss," he said, "for shooting at the fire!"

Full dark had fallen before they finished the meal, but before the earth had really got the feel of the soft blanket of shadows spread by the dying fingers of the day, a round yellow moon soared up over the edge of the world and drenched desert and rangeland with a flood of silver rain. It was so light that each mesquite thorn stood out like clear and bold tiny spears in the hands of elfin warriors.

The girl and the man rode the white blaze of the trail with the shimmer of the moonlight behind them and their shadows stretching long and black before. They rode silently for some time, held by the spell of beauty the moon's reflected fire wove over hill and mesa and rolling range. Their horses' irons rang loudly on the hard trail, the rippling echoes setting the coyotes to yipping and causing a venerable and hungry owl to bawl protest at the untimely interruption of his hunting.

"My name is Lonnie Garret," the girl told Hatfield. "I own the Bowtie spread . . . this is my range we're on now. Yes, I run it by myself. I have four hands. My mother died when I was born, and last year my father rode into Mexico and didn't ride back."

"Killed down there?"

"Worse," she replied, her lips tight with pain. "He and Brant Preston and another rancher, Craig Doyle, who owned the K8, rode into Mexico to get back some steers that were rustled from this side. They had three or four cowboys with them. Doyle said the cowboys were killed.

"Dad and Brant Preston were taken prisoner. Preston managed to escape from jail, but he could not get Dad out. He's still there. We've tried to get his release, but Cheno, the bandit, runs all that section of the country, and nobody can do anything with Cheno. I'm afraid Dad will die there."

Jim Hatfield nodded sympathetically, and the girl changed the subject.

"West of my range," she said, "between here and Cuevas

and on into the hills is *Don* Fernando Cartina's F Bar C, the biggest ranch in the county, and to the east is Brant Preston's Circle P."

"That's the range I rode over before I hit your spread, isn't it?" Hatfield interrupted.

"Yes, I imagine so," she replied, "that is, if you rode in from the east along the river. The range peters out into the desert farther east, but it's good land."

"Uhn-huh," Hatfield agreed. "Those deep coulées and cañons make good shelter from heat and snow. I imagine the grass stays good and uncovered almost all winter in those draws. Sort of a wide-looper's idea of heaven, though, if they operate in these parts."

"Yes," the girl said dryly. "The man who owns such a range has his hands full with rustlers, unless they happen to be friendly."

Jim Hatfield's dark brows lifted slightly, and he shot her a swift glance that she did not appear to notice.

"The Cingaro Trail runs across the Circle P," she commented with apparent irrelevance.

"Cingaro Trail?" Hatfield repeated after a short silence.

"Yes, the trail the smugglers and rustlers and robbers use to cross into Mexico. It runs north through Pardusco Cañon and on into New Mexico. Only the outlaws can follow it. In Pardusco Cañon it branches many times, and the branches run through side cañons and gorges and wind and twist until one who is unfamiliar with their windings is hopelessly lost.

"That is why it is so easy to run stock in this section and why stage robbers and murderers find so little difficulty in losing the sheriff when he rides after them. It is a terrible place, Pardusco Cañon. It's white with bones."

"The Gypsy Trail and Grizzly Cañon," the Ranger

translated, "shore sounds interestin'. Does the trail run any way near Cuevas?"

"Yes," Lonnie told him. "After passing across the Circle P range, it slants west across *Don* Fernando's F Bar C and enters the cañon. The cañon runs almost due west for quite a way and passes Cuevas about five miles to the north. There is said to be a trail out of Cuevas that enters the cañon, but if there is, nobody but the outlaws knows it."

"The Cingaro Trail crosses your spread, too, so then it would have to cross *Don* Fernando's," the Ranger remarked.

"No," the girl said. "*Don* Fernando's range bounds mine on the north. It also bounds the Circle P on the north. It is shaped like an L. My range and the Circle P run from the short side of the L to the river. The F Bar C is much larger than both our ranges put together."

"I see." Hatfield nodded. "*Don* Fernando must be the big he-wolf of these diggings."

"He's fine," the girl replied earnestly. "Old Spanish stock and a perfect gentleman. He is always doing things for the poorer people, and he pays his riders and his workers in the mine the best of wages and is very kind to them.

"He has only Mexicans riding for him, that is except Pierce Kimble, his foreman, but he employs Americans as well as Mexicans in his mine. You will like *Don* Fernando, if you meet him."

For a mile or more they rode in silence. Jim Hatfield was busy with his thoughts. *Brant Preston and that* Don *Fernando'll bear some investigating, it looks like,* he mused. *That Cingaro Trail business sounds interesting, too. Widelooping and dry-gulching gents have to go somewhere always, and, if you can manage to cut across the road they travel, it isn't hard to tangle their rope.*

V

"AS RODE THE KNIGHTS OF OLD"

The Ranger swiftly ran over what the girl had told him relative to the position of the various ranches and the town of Cuevas. From that information he constructed a map of the region in his mind.

All the information he had gathered so far corresponded very well with what he had learned during his talk with Captain McDowell. The territory formed roughly a right triangle, the longest side of which was the irregular line of the silvery river. The three spreads Lonnie Garret had mentioned were snugged in the angle.

To the north were other ranches, and to the west, chiefly on the far side of the range of hills, was the vestibule in which Cuevas was built. The big sawtooth mountains shouldered up north of the hills and near the New Mexico line. Beyond the strip of desert on the far side of the river loomed the purple mountains of Mexico.

It was a gloomily beautiful land, this vast stretch of rich range banded by strips of desert and slashed by cañon and gorge—beautiful and sinister. The Ranger, sensitive to the moods of a country as to those of men, could feel the tenseness and the threat that brooded over the moon-drenched landscape. No law west of the Pecos!

Here was the last frontier, the final stronghold of predatory forces that recognized no authority save that of their own desires. Evil things had happened recently in this dark and bloody land where the passions of diverse races clashed sharply, too many to be explained as mere sporadic outbursts of lawlessness.

Jim Hatfield instinctively knew that he was pitted against a ruthless organization of some kind, doubtless headed by one man or a small, closely aligned group that knew exactly what it wanted and was determined to get it and utterly indifferent as to what means were used just so they served. It was the kind of thing the Lone Wolf had gone up against before, but never to date had he encountered evidence of such brutality and callous cruelty.

Looks as if this gang, whoever they are, could teach the Comanches and Apaches things, he mused as they topped a swelling rise and saw the white ribbon of the trail tumble swiftly toward a distant dark blot that marked a spreading grove. His eyes narrowed slightly, and he stared at the shadowy oblong of the growth.

"I turn north just beyond the grove," the girl remarked, following the direction of his gaze. "What are you looking at?"

"Mebbe it's somebody coming to look for you," replied Hatfield, "several somebodies."

"I don't see anything," said Lonnie, staring perplexedly.

"You will soon as they ride outta the shadow," Jim Hatfield told her. "They left the trees a minute ago."

A moment later she exclaimed sharply. "Yes, I can see them now! What eyes you have."

"About a dozen or so, ridin' fast," the Ranger commented. Instinctively his slim right hand dropped to the butt of the heavy Colt snugged against his muscular thigh and loosened it slightly in its sheath. In the same flowing motion the reins were shifted to his right hand and the left-hand gun was touched lightly. So swift and casual had been the gesture that his companion did not notice. Her eyes were fixed on the tight group that rode swiftly up the trail to meet them.

On came the horsemen, riding with effortless ease, each seeming a part of the animal he bestrode. They numbered eleven, with one riding somewhat in advance, a tall man who swayed with lithe grace in his high-pommeled Mexican saddle.

Hatfield could see now that he wore the colorful garb of a *vaquero,* his serape sweeping across his broad breast, the moonlight glinting on silver conchos and spurs. The Ranger's keen glance also took in the rifle snugged in a saddle boot and the plain dark guns at his sinewy waist.

May be a Mexican, but he doesn't go in for pearl handles like so many of them do, he mused. *I'll bet I need just one guess to say who he is.*

A moment later his thin lips twitched into a grin of satisfaction at the girl's exclamation.

"Why, it's *Don* Fernando!"

She waved her hand and gave a call. The horsemen were now less than a hundred yards distant, thundering toward the pair, crowding every inch of the trail. Goldy snorted, and Jim Hatfield tensed. The Ranger gave a low whistle.

"That's ridin'," he applauded under his breath.

Less than a score of paces away the group came to a halt on sliding hoofs. Perfectly motionless, horse and man, they froze like statues while the tall leader rode slowly forward. His heavy sombrero swept low in salute, and he bowed with courtly grace. Hatfield expected a precise speech in stately Spanish. He was surprised at the easy, offhand greeting.

"Hello, Miss Garret," the Mexican began. "What are you doing out so late all by yourself?"

Don Fernando's speech was different from the careless drawl and slur of the American Texan, but he had not a trace of accent, nor the somewhat stilted choosing of words that usually marks the men of Spanish blood.

"I'm not alone." Lonnie smiled. "*Don* Fernando, this is Mister Jim Hatfield, who is looking for a job of riding. Mister Hatfield, *Don* Fernando Cartina, who I was telling you about."

"You'll have to excuse me, Mister Hatfield," said *Don* Fernando, his white teeth flashing under his small black mustache in an answering smile. "You see, when Miss Garret is around, I just naturally don't see anybody else."

"Can't say as I blame you, suh," agreed Hatfield as *Don* Fernando shook hands with a steely grip. To himself he said: *So damned good-looking he makes your eyes bat. All steel wire and whipcord. A real* hidalgo *or I've never seen one.*

"I stopped at your place," *Don* Fernando was saying to the girl. "Holly said you rode east early in the afternoon. I figured you'd ride back along the Cuevas Trail and took a chance on meeting you."

He wheeled his horse as he spoke and reined in beside Lonnie. The ranks of the *vaqueros* opened as they rode forward, and then closed in behind. Hatfield glanced across at *Don* Fernando, who was chatting lightly with the girl.

Fernando Cartina was handsome, astonishingly so. Tall, lithe, broad of shoulder and trim of waist, he was little darker than the bronzed Ranger. His hair was black and slightly inclined to curl. His eyes were large and flashing, his patrician features a cameo perfection of contour. A square jaw and firm mouth relieved his face of anything like a hint of effeminacy.

He held his head high with the pride of bearing of his race, but what resembled haughtiness was relieved by a smile of singular charm. It was a powerful face and an intelligent one. His lips were very thin, but finely formed. He nodded to Hatfield in a friendly way and addressed him.

"I can offer you a job in my mine, but I don't imagine it would interest you," he said. "I hire only *vaqueros* on my ranch, but I will be glad to recommend you to my friends. If you don't get anything, ride up to my *hacienda*, and I'll see what I can do."

The Ranger thanked *Don* Fernando, and, as the latter concentrated his attention on Lonnie Garret, the Ranger dropped back a pace or two until he was riding with the silent *vaqueros*. They glanced at him obliquely from their dark eyes but said nothing.

Mexicans with more Yaqui blood than Spanish, he decided after covertly studying them. *They're a plumb different brand from their boss. Top hands, no doubt about that, and mean as hungry Gila monsters if it becomes necessary. The kind the old* dons *of Mexico keep for their private armies. Reckon* Don *Fernando is pretty much Mexican in his way of thinking, even though he is Texas born and his pappy and grandpappy behind him. Salty* hombres, *those old* dons, *and Cartina's the same breed. I've got a hunch it'll be just too bad for the gents who're raising the hell around these diggings if he ever drops his loop on them.*

They reached the grove and rode through its dense shadows. As they reached the final fringe of growth on the far side, the Ranger's ear caught the rhythmical approach of a swiftly ridden horse. When they rode into the moonlight once more, the sounds had grown to a steady drum. Hatfield leaned forward in his saddle and peered ahead with interest.

A few hundred yards distant another trail cut at right angles the one they were riding. It flowed out of the jumble of hills to the north and wound south, soon plunging into a scattering of buttes and chimneys beyond which, only a few miles distant, was the yellow flood of the river. Along this trail, speeding toward the intersection, came a single horseman, superbly mounted. He leaned low over his horse's neck and urged the flying animal to greater effort. Like a specter in the moonlight he came, and like a specter he vanished among the grotesque spires to the south. The swift drum died to a whisper, the whisper to a blank emptiness. Only a patch of white foam, perishing in a clump of grass beside the main trail, remained as evidence that horse and rider had been real and not a figment of the imagination, born of the white moon and the blue shadows.

But in the instant of his passing, he had turned to gaze fully at the mounted group, and in that fleeting moment Jim Hatfield had a vision of a dark, sinister face rushing toward him out of the night—just such a glimpse as had been vouchsafed him on that other night of wind and rain and roaring storm. The concentration furrow was deep between his green eyes as he relaxed in his saddle once more.

"¡El Caballero! ¡El Caballero!" The name traveled through the ranks of the *vaqueros* in a tense, awed whisper.

Jim translated the exclamation: The Rider!

VI

"DEATH IN THE MOONLIGHT"

A mile farther on the trail branched. The main fork continued west; the other, a narrower and fainter track, ambled leisurely toward the north. Here the group pulled up. The girl urged Hatfield to spend the night at the Bowtie, but he declined.

"I wanna get a early start lookin' 'round when comes mawnin'," he explained.

"Well, this trail leads to my ranch house. Any time you feel like visiting the Bowtie, you know how to get there," invited Lonnie.

"And anybody will tell you how to get to the F Bar C," added *Don* Fernando.

Hatfield thanked them both and watched them vanish up the winding trail, riding very close together, their grim silent escort *tip-tupping* a few yards behind them.

They shore make a pair to draw to, mused the Ranger as he turned Goldy's head toward the distant glow that marked Cuevas. He grinned a little wryly and chuckled to himself. *A fine little gal,* he mused. *Wonder if that's why I can't seem to cotton to that good-lookin' jigger she's so darned interested in? Well, after all, bein' a Ranger doesn't keep a fellow from being human, and she is pretty as a spotted yearling.*

He laughed aloud and straightway forgot all about the red-haired girl and *Don* Fernando, his thoughts turning to the sinister figure of the mysterious Rider that had flashed past like some veiled phantom of the night. Ahead, lying like a leprous sore on a lovely face, appeared one of the strange bands of desert that striped the rich, grassy rangeland.

Butte and chimney and wind-gnawed spire rose grotesquely from the arid surface of shifting sands. Cholla cacti brandished their weird devil arms in the moonlight. Greasewood with white interlaced branches and inconspicuous greenish flowers loomed like the twisted skeletons of tortured ghosts. Once or twice Hatfield noted a pale glimmer that he knew to be the phosphorescent light that glowed in a skull. He shuddered in spite of himself, and Goldy snorted and twitched his skin.

Abruptly the Ranger pulled the yellow horse to a halt. His mouth suddenly dry, a moist clamminess was reeking his palms. He sat and stared at the thing of blasted horror from which the moonlight seemed to shudder away.

"God!" he breathed between his teeth. "Hearin' about it and seein' it is mighty different!"

Gaunt, sinister, a gigantic cholla cactus reared beside the trail, and, crucified among the needle-sharp spines, was what had once been a man. Now he was a thing to make the very coyotes and desert snakes shrink away.

Broken, twisted, caked with dried blood, the motionless form still vividly portrayed the awful writhings of unthinkable agony. The face was a tortured mask that seemed to scream with silent voice and glare with eyeless sockets at the passionless stars.

Steeling himself, the Ranger rode closer, and, as he peered at the pitiful remains, his green eyes grew cold as a gray winter sea and in their depths flickered little smoky flames like fire under ice. The man was dead but a few hours at most. Perhaps less than a full sixty minutes had passed since he had screamed out his life in blood and horror.

In the Lone Wolf's brain was a beat as of a soft hammer—such a sound as is made by swift hoofs speeding across desert sand. Before his eyes flickered a vision on a sinister dark face rushing toward him out of the night.

"El Caballero," he repeated. Lean jaw set like iron, he turned his horse's head again toward the distant glow that was Cuevas. "Yeah, those are the hellions I have business with . . . those damn' riders! Them and that jigger the old *peón* called El Hombre."

The glow of Cuevas became myriad of twinkles, and the air quivered with the steady, monotonous pound of the mining town's never-resting stamp mills. Soon the twinkles were the lighted squares of many windows, and the pound

of the stamps was but the undertone of the squalling roar
that surged up from saloons, gambling hells, dance halls,
and pleasure palaces. There, men who rode the green
rangeland, and men who burrowed in the depths of the
lurid earth, relieved hard toil with harder pleasure. There
they gave no thought to tomorrow and looked death in the
face and told him to go about his business and be damned.

Even as the Ranger rode slowly along the crowded main
street in search of shelter and provender for his weary
cayuse, another rider tore into town from the north, his
horse's coat reeking with sweat and white with foam. Dark
of face, furtive of eye, he paused before a dimly lighted
cantina that huddled in the very shadow of the gaunt mine
buildings.

He left his spent broncho standing with wide-spread legs
and hanging head and slipped through a rear door of the
ramshackle saloon. A hard-faced bartender caught his
glance, and nodded toward a corner table, beside which sat
other dark men with wide sombreros pulled low over their
eyes and glasses of fiery tequila in their hands. For tense
moments the high crowns of the sombreros huddled closely
together; voices sounded terse gutturals.

Suddenly, one by one, four lithe figures left the table and
vanished through the black rectangle of the door. Left behind was a single man whose arm was swathed in bandages,
but whose eyes glowed with an unholy light while he licked
his thin lips as if in pleasurable anticipation.

A newcomer sauntered across the room and dropped
into one of the vacant chairs. "You smile, Pedro," he remarked in greeting. "Your thoughts . . . they are pleasant?"

"*Sí*," nodded the other grimly. "*Sí*. I think . . . of re-
venge!"

"Ha!" The questioner's voice was understanding. He cast a significant glance at the bandaged arm. "A knife. A bullet?"

"No," returned the injured man savagely. "A horse!"

The Ranger found a livery stable and turned Goldy over to a yawning hostler after seeing to it personally that the sorrel was properly cared for. Then he walked unhurriedly onto the main street again and looked up a restaurant.

"I hanker to surround a double portion of hog's hip and cackle berries," he told the bland Chinaman who waited on him.

"Can do," smiled the Chinaman. "Put up top-side fire. You like um eggs bottom side top or under?"

"Whatever you say," Jim sighed resignedly. "I'm not gonna get in any argument with you about it. You twirl your loop, and I'll rear back and tie fast."

"Can do," agreed the Chinaman. "Cook um two times twice, bottom, too."

After finishing his meal, Jim sat smoking and thinking of his next move. He decided to avoid Sheriff Jed Raines for the present. The Lone Wolf was averse to seeking assistance at any time. In this instance, he shrewdly deduced that he would get little of any value from the sheriff. Hatfield had read between the lines of the peace officer's letter and realized that the bluff old frontiersman was utterly unfit to cope with such a situation as had arisen in his county. It was a Ranger job, and the Rangers didn't make a practice of asking for help. *I'll just play a lone hand for a spell* was his decision.

Pinching out his smoke, he left the restaurant and strolled along the busy street. Late though the hour was, every saloon was crowded. Orchestras bellowed and boots thumped. Voices bawled song; other voices bawled curses. It was hard to tell which were the more unmusical. The high-pitched laughter of women cut through the deep rumble of the men.

Wonder if they do this every night, or is it payday or something? Jim asked himself. He entered a brilliantly lighted saloon, unaware that dark eyes watched him pass through the swinging doors—eyes that smoldered with hate, in the depths of which was a look of fixed purpose. He found a place at the long bar and ordered whisky. Glass in hand he leaned across the bar and surveyed the room.

It was big and crowded, with a dance floor at one end, a couple of roulette wheels and a number of poker tables, all going full blast. On his high stool perched the look-out, a sawed-off shotgun across his knees, his glance flickering from table to table, alert for arguments that might become serious or a quick raid on the stacks of gold pieces resting beside the elbow of each banker. The air of the place was a tolerant, but reckless one.

Sort of like open kegs of gunpowder setting around in a hot kitchen, Hatfield decided, finishing his drink and calling for another. Studying the groups at the various tables, the Ranger's attention was attracted by a poker game that was in progress not far from the bar. Five men sat in, quiet, low-spoken men who appeared intent on their game, but whose eyes flickered up from their cards each time the swinging doors creaked on their hinges.

The big room was well sprinkled with Mexicans in velvet and silver and gay serapes, but the five at the table were obviously Texans, although one who, Hatfield quickly noted, appeared to dominate the group was as dark of complexion as the swarthy men from below the line. A second glance told the Ranger, however, that his eyes instead of being black were so darkly blue as to appear black and were fringed with sooty lashes. His hair was as jet as Hatfield's and slightly inclined to curl. Hard of eye and hard of mouth, he was above middle height, slim, and lithe. The Ranger studied the man's dark, slightly sinister face, his own black brows drawing slightly together. There was something familiar about it, something unpleasantly reminiscent.

I haven't ever seen that jigger before, he mused, *leastwise not as I can recollect, but he shore reminds me of somebody I have seen somewhere. Him and the rest of the outfit is salty-looking enough, all right. Wonder who they are?*

The doors creaked, and the men at the table looked up quickly. They were seated so that each member could see the doors without turning around, which fact was not lost on the Ranger. He also glanced in the direction of the doors.

Four men had just entered, Mexicans, undoubtedly, with Yaqui blood predominating. Their sombreros were pulled low, and their black eyes glinted in the shadow of the broad brims. In a compact group they moved across the room and lined up at the bar on Hatfield's left. They did not even glance at him as they ordered tequila and paid for it with a gold piece.

Hatfield took no notice of them apparently, but out of the corner of his eye he watched them in the mirror of the back-bar and saw the thin lips of the man nearest to him move in an inaudible remark. The man raised his filled glass toward his lips and in doing so managed to strike it against the Ranger's shoulder. The fiery liquor splashed back into his face and spilled over his gaudy serape, leaving a dark stain on the blanket's bright surface. The move had all the appearances of an accident, but the Ranger knew that it was

116

intentional on the man's part, perfectly timed and calculated. With lazy grace he turned to face the other, who let out a Spanish curse.

"¡Caramba! I am insult!" the Mexican bawled. "You knock the drink to my face! You look for fight!"

Like a blur of dark light his hand flashed down and up, but even as the knife gleamed, Hatfield hit him right and left and sent him crashing in a senseless heap to the floor. Instantly his companions yelled their rage and went for guns and knives. The room seemed to explode with the roar of six-shooters.

Weaving, ducking, side-stepping backward until he was against the wall, Hatfield hammered the group with bullets. He downed one man, smashed the shoulder of a second, and shot the gun from the hand of the third. Blood streaming from a gashed cheek, holes in his hat and shirt sleeves, he crouched behind his smoking guns, his cold green eyes sweeping the room, which was in a pandemonium.

Yells, curses, the screams of women, and the bellows of the look-out filled the air. The man Hatfield had hit raised his head dazedly and glared about. Intelligence returned with a rush, and he whipped out his gun. The Ranger shot him as across the room there went up a howl of anger. The Mexicans there were rallying to the call of blood.

"Keel!" "Kill the gringo!" "¡Maldito!" "Keel!"

Hatfield swept the room with a swift glance. The door was blocked hopelessly, so were the windows, all save one, a side window to his right, but there was a score of feet of open floor to cover before he could hope to reach it.

The Ranger noticed in his quick glance that the group of Texans at the table were on their feet, staring at him in amazement. Their hands were on their guns, but they made no move of any sort. Guns were banging across the room. Bullets whined past the Ranger.

Suddenly both his heavy Colts tipped up. Fire streamed from the black muzzles. One of the big hanging lamps slam-jingled against the ceiling. A second was blasted from its moorings and hit the floor in a shower of sparks and oil. Out went the third and last lamp. Darkness blanketed the room.

The Ranger slammed his guns into their holsters, went across the open floor space like a drifting shadow, and through the side window in a crashing dive. Behind him sounded a terrific bedlam of yells, howls, curses, and shots. He hit the dusty ground of a dark alley, rolled over, and came to his feet like a cat as a form thudded in the dust beside him.

Hatfield's Colt flashed out, and the long barrel jammed into the stomach of the man as the latter staggered erect. By the shimmer of the moonlight he recognized the swarthy man who had dominated the group at the poker table.

"Don't shoot, stranger," the man gasped. "We hadda get out, too. There's fifty greasers in there b'ilin' for a kill. Here come my boys . . . let four out and shoot the next one."

Hatfield slewed in behind the other as dark figures poured through the smashed window.

"C'mon," growled a deep bass voice. "We 'uns is all out. C'mon 'fore that damn' ol' fool of a sheriff and his dep'ty gets here and wants to lock somebody up. He'll blame we 'uns for what all happened. C'mon."

"Yeah, you c'mon, too, stranger," urged the dark-faced man. "Pen that hawgleg and come 'long with us. I'll lay to it you ain't hankerin' to be locked up, either."

Jim Hatfield's mind was working at lightning speed.

Without hesitation he shoved his gun back into its sheath.

"Hell, no," he agreed. "I'll say I ain't. Where you goin'?"

"To my ranch!" yelled the other as a shotgun boomed through the window opening and buckshot spattered them with dust. "C'mon!"

Down the alley they raced, with the shotgun booming behind them.

"Gotta get my hoss," Hatfield panted. "Watson's stable."

"Right around the next corner," gasped the dark man. "Hustle, feller, we gotta get outta this."

During the run down the alley, Hatfield had made up his mind. These men had no desire to come to grips with the law. Why, he didn't know, but the fact that they didn't want to was important. One of the Lone Wolf's axioms was: You can't find out crooked things by associating with straight people. When you're hunting snakes, go where snakes hang out.

Without hesitation he saddled Goldy and led him from the stable. Outside, others were waiting, already mounted, their horses champing impatiently.

"You shore raised hell and shoved a chunk under a corner, feller," said the swarthy leader as they rode off. "Listen to 'em bawl up there!"

"Uhn-huh, and you sot the damn' hawg-waller on fire when you busted them lamps," growled the owner of the deep bass. "Betcha me ol' Raines rides out with warrants for all of us t'morrer. Look at 'er blaze!"

"Not a chance," replied the leader. " 'Cause the man who owns the place ain't gonna make no complaint! He'll jest report a fight 'tween jiggers he don't know. See, they're gettin' the fire out, too. Well, c'mon, you jughaids, let's sift sand."

Through a maze of crooked, evil-smelling alleys the swarthy man led the way. Soon the hard, white surface of the trail unrolled before them. Hatfield found himself riding swiftly back over the way by which he had entered town earlier in the night. The swarthy man reined back beside him.

"Feller, with a gun you're a whizzer," he admired. "It ain't none of my business why them hellions wanted to cash you in, and I ain't askin' the reason. Fact is, I'm askin' you jest one question . . . you passin' through, or are you aimin' on hangin' 'round these diggin's for a spell?"

The Ranger tried to read his face, but the moon was low in the sky now and the night too dark.

"All depends," he replied, "I'm sorta trailin' my rope at present . . . out of a job."

"Fine!" exclaimed the other. "I can use a hand like you. Be plumb pleased to sign you up if you're agreeable."

"All right," Hatfield told him. "I'll give you a whirl. What did you say your outfit is?"

"The Circle P, over to the east," replied the other. "I'm Brant Preston!"

VII

"THE WELL OF SILENCE"

Dawn was streaking the sky with rose and gold and flaming scarlet when they reached the white adobe buildings of the Circle P. Thoroughly tired out, the Ranger tumbled into the bunk assigned him in the bunkhouse and went to sleep.

The others were not slow in following his example. None of them saw the lithe, furtive man who slipped silently out of the grove back of the ranch house, entered the building, and soon afterward departed as silently as he had come.

When Hatfield awoke, Curly Wilkes, the big man with the bass voice, was sitting on the foot of his bunk.

"The boss wants you to come up to the house," Wilkes said, "wants to talk with you. Yeah," in answer to Hatfield's unspoken question, "there's a nice big trough in back you can take a bath in. Go ahaid, no wimmen folks 'round hereabout. Nice water. I had a bath in there come a month next Sat'day . . . didn't find but three frawgs."

The Ranger had his bath without disturbing any frogs. Puffing on a swiftly rolled cigarette, he strolled up to the front door of the big, white ranch house.

He found the ranch owner eating breakfast. Preston waved a hospitable hand to a chair on the opposite side of the table.

"Set, and get on the outside of a helpin' of chuck," he invited. "I jest hired a new cook a hour or so ago, and he shore knows how to rustle vittles. My last one was a Mex woman with seven kids. She up and marries a widower with nine. Time they get started in bus'ness themselves, they'd oughta have a right pert family.

"The jigger I jest took on talks like a scrambled aig, but scrambles aigs till you think they's jest laid this mawnin', 'stead of havin' to be hit with a meat axe to stop 'em crowin'."

The kitchen door opened, and a plate of golden eggs and fragrant fried bacon came in. With them was a bland Chinaman. Not so bland, however, as when Hatfield had seen him the night before in the Cuevas restaurant. One eye was partially closed and beautifully ringed with blue. His nose was scratched, and his lips had a puffy look.

"Howdy," greeted the Ranger mildly. "How come you aren't at the restaurant?"

"Boss comes in without wife," explained the celestial. "Wife she hit kletchup bottle with me . . . hit chair with boss. Me quit before something hlappen."

"Hell, you look like you didn't quit soon enough. But how come the boss's wife cut up all this shindig when you just said he come in without her?"

"Boss, he come in flont dloor with redhead dance-hall girl. Boss's wife clome in back door with shotgun. Me say boss gone before he clome in. She say . . . 'You liar!' She right!"

"Calculate you did best not to argue with her," agreed Hatfield. "Say, this ham is shore prime."

"Me cook squeal outta pig and makeum sweet like music," nodded the Chinaman as he headed for the door.

"I shore b'lieve you could," admitted Preston. "By the way, what's your name, so's I can put it on the payroll."

"Me Hang Soon," replied the new cook.

"Wouldn't be a mite surprised," countered Preston. "Anyhow, you're honest 'bout it. Most folks won't admit it."

Preston turned to Hatfield as the Chinaman vanished after more biscuits.

"Got a few things to tell you," he said. "Fust off, if you sign up with me, you're signin' up with a mighty unpopular outfit. Most folks hereabouts ain't got much use for the Circle P. Sheriff Raines 'cuses us of bein' responsible for the wide-loopin' and other hell-raisin' what's been goin' on of late. Says he's jest waitin' till he gets proof 'fore he cracks down on us.

"So far he ain't got none, but you never can tell what'll happen in this deestrict. Fact is, I got a notion he'd already took a chanct on us if it weren't for *Don* Fernando Cartina tellin' him not to go off half-cocked. Cartina . . . he's the biggest owner hereabouts . . . is square and decent, even if he has got plenty greaser blood, and he don't make no moves 'less he's shore of what he's doin'.

"Some gents in this neck of the woods ain't jest that way. Wat Fisher of the Skyrocket and Ben Warms of the Bar W is purty hotheaded. The day they found a batch of Skyrocket and Bar W calves corralled in Red Rim Cañon, which is up to the nawtheast corner of my spread, they was all set to ride over here and have it out with me and the boys, even though they didn't have no proof that the Circle P had anythin' to do with them dogies bein' there.

"Cartina talked 'em outta it . . . told 'em not to take the law in their own hands. Him and his foreman, Pierce Kimble, had quite an arg'fying 'bout it. Pierce said Fisher and Warms had the right idea and was for throwin' in with 'em. *Don* Fernando saved a hefty passel of trouble that day.

"The Skyrocket and Bar W outfits is plenty salty, and my boys ain't 'zactly what you'd call daisy pickers. I sorta make it a practice to hire hands what is willin' to back the spread up if come nec'sary . . . but I allus tell 'em what they're up against so's they can pull out in time if they're a mind to."

"That's square enough," Jim Hatfield admitted. "Well, many border outfits are salty. I've worked with one or two myself that didn't go to Sunday school regular. You pay average wages?"

"I pays a little better than most," Preston replied. "There's one other little thing I wanna mention," he added, his dark blue eyes inscrutable, his face wooden in its lack of expression.

"Yeah?"

"Uhn-huh . . . I had some trouble down Mexico way. They thought I was a rustler."

"Hell, it's a wonder you came out of it alive," was the Ranger's only comment.

For an instant Preston's eyes flickered slightly, and a crease appeared between his dark brows. His glance was speculative as it rested on the Lone Wolf's bronzed face. He started to speak, hesitated, apparently changed his mind. What he did say, Hatfield felt sure, was not what he had at first intended.

"All right," he said brusquely, "I'll sign you up soon as we finish eatin'. You can ride out with Wilkes and get the low-down on the spread."

Over his cigarette, Hatfield mentioned that he had encountered Lonnie Garret and *Don* Fernando Cartina in the course of his ride toward Cuevas, refraining from going into detail as to the meeting. "That little redhead is shore a pretty gal," he added.

Preston's black brows drew together, and there was a smoldering glow in his eyes. He opened his lips, and shut them tightly again. Once more Hatfield felt that he did not speak his first thought.

"Yeah, she is," Preston said.

At the door, before going out to join Carly Wilkes at the bunkhouse, the Ranger paused.

"Last night, when I was amblin' along with *Don* Fernando's *vaqueros*, I heard them making a funny gabble about some jigger they called The Rider . . . seemed all het up over him. You any notion what they meant?"

For a second time Brant Preston's black lashes flickered. His dark, slightly sinister face grew bleak and worried.

"Feller," he said softly, "there's some things in this district that it ain't overly healthy to gab 'bout too much. That there Rider gent is one of 'em."

124

★ ★ ★ ★ ★

In the company of Curly Wilkes, Jim Hatfield rode north and east over Preston's range. Curly pointed out the location of streams and water holes, cañons and draws, and other items with which a new hand should become familiar.

The Ranger quickly decided that the Circle P was a good range, despite the proximity of the desert on the east and hilly formations to the north. Late in the afternoon Wilkes led the way to a clearly defined trail that always seemed to thread its way through gorge and ravine and seek the shadow of overhanging cliff or dense thicket. It was a furtive track that shunned the open sunlight and hurried toward the dark shelter of the northern hills.

"This's the Cingaro Trail," remarked Wilkes. "There's folks what say the devil swished it out with his tail in the fust place. Can't say as to that, but it's shore helped to keep hell workin' overtime ever since it was fust rode. You ever hear tell of it?"

He seemed to stare straight at his horse's ears as he asked the question, but Jim Hatfield caught the glimpse of his eyes slanting toward their corners.

"Uhn-huh," the Ranger replied readily, "seems that little redhead, Miss Garret, said somethin' about it when I was ridin' with her and *Don* Fernando last night. I never heard of it before. You see," he added, "I rode from over east . . . haven't ever been this far south and west in Texas before. Before this, I worked on a spread over Silver Valley way. Before that I rode in the Alamita Basin country and around about the Llano River. I was with old man Hogadorn's Hashknife spread in the river country."

Curly nodded soberly. "I've heard of the Hashknife outfit," he admitted. "Usta know a feller what worked for it. He said Hogadorn was a square *hombre* but a salty one.

Outfit was sorta salty, too. Fellers there had lotsa run-ins with other jiggers."

Hatfield grinned back of his lips. He knew that Wilkes was itching with curiosity about the fight in the Cuevas saloon. He also knew that the big cowpuncher would never ask outright why apparently wanton murder had been attempted. Looking straight ahead, he made what sounded like an irrelevant remark.

"I rode for a spell in Mexico," he said softly. "Rode north again mighty fast one day, too."

Curly Wilkes nodded his understanding. More than one cowpuncher had ridden out of Mexico with a blood feud on his hands. Just as often as not, the feud caught up with him north of the Río Grande, with disastrous results to himself or to those who rode on his trail.

For some time they continued in silence toward the dark jumble of hills that was the Circle P's northern boundary, Hatfield slightly in the lead. Directly ahead the trail slanted up a long rise to an irregular rim aflame with the saffron flame of the low-lying sun.

Hatfield deftly rolled a cigarette with the slim fingers of one hand. There was a dry buzz from a clump of grass alongside the trail, and Goldy shied away from the rattler's menace. The quick jolt spun the finished cigarette from Jim's grasp. He dived to retrieve it before it fluttered to the ground, swinging low over the sorrel's neck.

Cr-r-r-rack! Thud!

Jim felt a blast of wind against the back of his neck as the bullet yelled through the space his body had occupied the instant before. A queer little grunt followed the hard *smack* of it against flesh and bone. Curly Wilkes raised on his toes in the stirrups and pitched sideward from the saddle.

In a single streaking movement Hatfield was off his

horse. His rifle was in his hands before his feet hit the ground. A split second later he was hammering the sullenly flaring rim of the rise with bullets where his keen eyes had caught the pale blue spiral of a tiny wisp of smoke.

There was no answer to his fire. Shoving fresh cartridges into the magazine, he crouched back of his horse, eyes never leaving the rim, sweeping it back and forth for the least sign of movement or telltale glint of metal. For a long minute the Ranger waited, tense and ready, then he stepped quickly from behind the horse and back again in the same lithe movement.

Still the rim was silent.

I either drilled him or he scooted right after he pulled trigger, he decided. *Calculate he figured he couldn't miss and didn't even wait to see what happened.*

A single glance at the still form in the dust of the trail told him that, although the unseen dry-gulcher had missed his intended mark, he had nevertheless garnered a victim. A neat, round hole was in Curly Wilkes's chest.

Hatfield glanced at the clump of grass, now devoid of its grisly tenant, that had evidently glided away among the rocks.

"Never calculated I'd ever be sayin' much obliged to a snake, but I guess I am," he remarked. "If it hadn't been for that fellow buzzing and scaring the daylights out of Goldy, that other sidewinder up there wouldn't've missed what he aimed at."

Wilkes's well-trained horse still stood motionlessly. "I'll come back for you in a minute," Hatfield promised, patting the faithful animal's neck. Swiftly he rode up the trail until he was within fifty yards of the glowering rim. Here he dismounted and covered the remaining distance on foot, rifle ready. Finally he peered over the lip.

The trail tumbled steeply down the far side of the rise to plunge into a dark cañon mouth a half mile distant, between whose gloomy walls the dry-gulcher had doubtless vanished. For some time Hatfield studied the vista of forbidding hills and gorges. Then, satisfied that no immediate danger lay in that direction, he carefully went over the ground.

Hatfield found where the killer had crouched behind a boulder, and where he had left his horse. The hoof marks of the latter showed worn irons with no peculiarity of marking. Still the Ranger searched with keen eyes. At last he found what he had hoped the dry-gulcher in his haste to escape might have left behind. It was more than he had hoped for.

Glinting in a clump of grass was an exploded cartridge case. Beside it was an unfired cartridge. Hatfield stared at them with narrowing eyes. His lean face wore a pleased expression as he carefully stowed them away in an inside pocket.

"Full better'n I'd hoped," he exulted. "Not much to go on, but less'n this has hanged a jigger before now. No wonder he hightailed after jest taking one shot."

For several minutes he studied the distant cañon mouth. Then he turned and strode back to his waiting sorrel. He loaded the body of Curly Wilkes onto his horse, fastened it securely, and set out for the Circle P ranch house, leading the burdened animal. Of necessity, he rode slowly.

There was no such hindrance, however, for the man who tore along the snaky Cingaro Trail, spurring his reeking horse and cursing the rifle that was snugged in his saddle boot. He also cursed his own neglect.

"That's what I get for puttin' things off," he grated. He glanced at the westering sun and made a quick mental calculation.

"Time to stop and put Pedro and Miguel on the job," he muttered. "Yeah, that's the idea. *They* won't slip!"

He lashed the straining horse with his quirt and chuckled evilly, his eyes hot with anticipation.

VIII

"ROBBER'S RUSE"

Old John Doan, driver of the Crater-Cuevas stage, heaved a sigh of relief as the clumsy coach rolled out of shadowy Lobo Cañon and onto the fairly open stretch of desert that lay between the Zarzal Hills and the Cuevas rangeland. Bert Livesay, the shotgun guard, also felt better. In the stage strongbox was the payroll for the Cuevas mines, and other specie, totaling more than thirty thousand dollars.

Of course, the shipment from Crater to the Cuevas bank was made in the strictest secrecy, but you never could tell, and Lobo Cañon was an ideal spot for a hold-up. Out in the open, with the trail winding ahead clear, with only an occasional grove or clump of mesquite to break the monotony, was much better.

"Calculate I can take time out for a smoke," remarked Livesay, reaching for the makings. Old John rumbled something unintelligible, his deep-set gray eyes on the trail ahead. Livesay had half finished his cigarette when the driver grunted sharply.

"Somethin' 'longside the road this side that clump of mesquite," he said.

Livesay saw it, too, a crouching something that at first puzzled him.

"Hell!" he exclaimed suddenly. "It's a dead hoss and a

coupla fellers. See, one of 'em's layin' on the ground and t'other's bendin' over him. Looks like somebody's been hurt."

"Looks thataway," agreed the driver, "but we ain't takin' no chances. Get that scatter-gun of yours handy."

Livesay cocked his shotgun and laid it across his knees. He peered sharply at the queer group as the stage sped down the low rise. It was but a hundred yards distant when the crouching figure turned.

The man's face was a bloody smear. The features were indistinguishable as such. He swayed on his knees, and tried to stagger erect. They could see now that the man who lay prone was also covered with blood. The horse that lay by the side of the road had a broken leg, the white splintered bone protruding through the skin. A little distance away, another horse stood with hanging head and widespread legs, apparently in the last stages of exhaustion.

Old John's hand tightened on the reins.

The kneeling man opened his bloody mouth. "Help!" he croaked, and collapsed across the motionless body of his companion.

Throwing his weight against the reins, old John pulled the stage to a jingling halt. His passengers, two elderly drummers, peered through the window with anxious faces.

"You keep a eye on things," John Doan told the guard. "I'll see what I can do for them fellers."

He got down stiffly, and stumped forward. Stooping over the injured man, he tried to lift him from the flaccid body of his companion, but the weight was too great for his strength.

"Gimme a hand, Bert," he called. "This 'n' 'pears to be still alive . . . t'other one's jest soaked with blood."

Livesay laid his shotgun on the seat and swung down.

130

The unconscious man was groaning pitifully. His companion lay without sound or movement. Livesay bent down to assist Doan.

Like a released spring, the "injured" man came to his feet. His fist crashed against the old driver's jaw, and knocked him down. Livesay, astounded recognition popping his eyes and sagging jaw, went for his gun.

The "dead" man on the ground galvanized to instant action. His hand flickered like a striking snake, and he shot from the hip, smashing the guard in the stomach and breast with heavy slugs. Livesay went down, gasping and retching. Old John Doan was struggling to his feet. A bullet took him squarely, and he crumpled up beside the dying guard.

The terror-stricken passengers heard the drum of swift hoofs. From the mesquite thicket down the trail burst two riders, one leading a spare horse. They swept up to the stage, their eyes glinting through the holes in the black masks they wore.

"Haul that box out," one curtly ordered the two passengers. He swung to the ground as the trembling men hastened to obey. From his saddlebags he took a hammer and a cold chisel. A few blows knocked the lid off the box. Working with swift efficiency, the four robbers transferred the gold and bills from the box to their saddlebags.

"All right," the leader told the passengers, "if either of you can drive, you can take this contraption inter town. If you can't, you'll hafta wait till somebody comes 'long and picks you up. ¡Adiós!"

Securing the shotgun, rifle, and sixes of the slain guard and driver, the grim quartet mounted, the "injured" man forking the exhausted horse, which was not so exhausted as it appeared. Without a glance at their murdered victims, they rode into the dark mouth of Lobo Cañon.

"S . . . see that dead horse?" The taller of the two passengers was speaking in a quavering voice. "Its throat has been cut. That's where they got the blood to smear on their faces. God, I'm sick!"

His companion, of a sterner mold, walked over to the silent bodies. "Come on and help me put them in the coach," he said. "Yes, I can drive a little . . . enough to keep this damn' hearse on the road. Hurry, it's nearly dark."

As the stagecoach rumbled along with its ghastly occupants, another rider was traveling along with a ghostly companion. Hatfield was returning to the Circle P with the stiffening body of Curly Wilkes.

Night had long fallen when the Ranger reached the ranch. The bunkhouse was dark, and a single light showed where Hang Soon pottered about the ranch house kitchen. It was very shadowy under the trees that shaded the bunkhouse.

Hatfield dismounted and, taking Wilkes's body in his arms, headed for the bunkhouse. The door was ajar. He kicked it open and entered. He tensed as he thought he glimpsed stealthy movement.

Out of the dark interior gushed a lance of flame. The walls rocked to the roar of a gun. The Ranger reeled back under the terrific impact of the heavy slug, his heel caught on the doorsill, and he sprawled on the ground. Through the doorway leaped two shadowy figures, hissing exultant curses.

Prone on the ground, the Lone Wolf drew and fired from the hip, the explosions of his gun blending in a single deafening roar of sound. The foremost figure crumpled up like a sack of old clothes, and just as silently. The second man yelled shrill agony as he went down. Whirling over sideward, Hatfield drew his other gun and grimly hammered the prostrate forms with bullets. Then he got stiffly to his feet, lean face set, eyes bleakly cold.

Inside the ranch house Jim Hatfield could hear Hang Soon's squalling screeches and the scampering of his slippered feet.

"Bring a light, Hang!" he shouted. "It's me, Hatfield. Rustle a hoof, you jughead."

"Me bling shotgun!" howled Hang. "Me blow loose flom under hat!"

"Leave that scatter-gun be!" roared Hatfield. "If you start pullin' trigger, the only safe place'll be behind you!"

A moment later Hang Soon came pattering through the door with a lantern, sputtering something that sounded to Jim Hatfield like firecrackers going off in a rain barrel.

The Ranger took the lantern, but he did not first turn to the two men he had shot. He felt reasonably sure they would stay where they were. Instead, he bent over the grotesquely sprawled form of Curly Wilkes.

There was a second hole in Wilkes's chest now, a futile-looking hole with in-sinking edges, from which no blood oozed. A whitish glimpse of shattered breastbone showed.

Damned lucky for me the slug hit him in the thickest part, Jim Hatfield told himself grimly. *If I hadn't had him in my arms in front of me, he and I'd both be lying down, saying nothing. Reckon it was so dark under the trees they didn't notice the two horses. Grass is mighty thick, and they couldn't tell from hearing that two sets of hoofs were working. Calculate when they saw me tumble backward, they thought they'd done for me. Wonder if they were waiting for me or somebody else?*

"Let's see if we can find where they left their hosses," he remarked to the chattering Chinaman. "They must have . . . ," he began, and suddenly paused, his lean body tense.

"Hoss what ain't here come," gurgled Hang Soon apprehensively.

"Uhn-huh, comin' fast, too. Douse that lantern and get back out of sight under the trees."

Hang Soon hastened to obey. The Ranger glided to his horse and pulled his heavy rifle from the boot. Hidden in the shadows he waited, his eyes on the trail that leaped from the blackness of a grove a few hundred yards distant. Moonlight was flooding in now, and it glowed whitely like cooling liquid silver.

Four horsemen burst from the grove and rode swiftly toward the ranch house. Hatfield peered with narrowed eyes, noting the coats of the animals dark with sweat and flecked with patches of foam. He stepped from the shadows and called a greeting. A moment later, Brant Preston and his three cowboys—Crowley, Kearns, and Hilton—where dismounting in front of the bunkhouse.

"What the hell's goin' on?" demanded the Circle P owner. "We heard shootin' and hustled to get here."

Jim Hatfield told them briefly, with no waste of words. As he related the circumstances of Curly Wilkes's death, he read suspicion and distrust in the hard eyes of the three cowpunchers. Preston's dark face was inscrutable. When Hatfield had finished, he knelt down and examined the body of Wilkes by the lantern that Hang Soon had relighted. He gave particular attention to the chest wounds. Finally he nodded and got to his feet.

"Judging from what I've seen of folks that've been shot, and I've seen quite a few, poor old Curly got his shot in jest 'bout the way you mentioned," Preston said. "He was shot by somebody from quite a ways off and up 'bove him, and with a big-caliber rifle, or I'm a heap mistook. Ain't no doubt 'bout that other shot bein' got after he was dead.

Now does anybody know these gents Hatfield perf'rated?"

"They're greasers," said Crowley, a grim, taciturn little man with a drooping mustache.

"Mostly Injun blood," amended lantern-jawed Hank Hilton. "Nope, I ain't seen neither of 'em before. Hev you, Tart?"

Tart Kearns, whose mild blue eyes were as deceptive as was his slight frame, shook his head wordlessly. Tart seldom said anything, but when he did, it was listened to.

"You can see what you've let yourself in for, Hatfield," remarked Brant Preston. "Wilkes makes the third man I've had killed in the past two months . . . and never knowed who did the killin'. This is the fust time we've ever seen hide or hair of any of the hellions."

"Mebbe this'll end it. Mebbe these are the jiggers who've been kickin' up all the hell," Hatfield offered tentatively.

Preston swore a deep-chested oath. "No chance," he growled. "These skulkin' skunks is jest a coupla hired hands. There's somebody else back of this . . . somebody with brains."

Then Wes Crowley drawled what seemed an utterly irrelevant remark: "I seed Pierce Kimble in town last night. He grinned at me."

Again Hatfield sensed a sudden stiffening of the group. Preston broke harshly into the silence. "Wes," the cowman's voice cracked like a whip, "you know nobody's got anythin' 'gainst Kimble what would c'nect him with sich doin's as this. He's a killer, yeah, and the fastest gunslinger in these parts, but that don't mean a feller's a thief and a murderer. 'Sides, you know *Don* Fernando wouldn't keep anybody on what was that kinda *hombre*."

"*Don* Fernando ain't past bein' fooled," retorted Crowley grimly. "I ain't got no use for that dead-faced ta-

135

rantula, and I never will have. When he grins at me, that slow, creepin' grin of his'n, damned if I don't get the shivers . . . jest like a goose had walked over where my grave is gonna be."

Hatfield glanced swiftly at the hard-bitten little man. He had a feeling that all Wes Crowley knew about fear was the murky idea conveyed to him by the dictionary definition, that is, if Wes had ever seen the inside of a dictionary, which he doubted. The frank admission that Pierce Kimble gave him an unpleasant feeling aroused an intense curiosity in the Ranger as to just what Kimble was like.

The group shifted uncomfortably at Crowley's words. Even the more intelligent Preston seemed ill at ease. He spoke hurriedly, with an evident desire to change the subject.

"The sheriff''ll hafta know 'bout these killin's," he said. "If we don't say nothin' 'bout 'em, it'll look suspicious. We could pitch them damn' greasers in a hole, and it would be all right, but folks is gonna ask questions 'bout Curly Wilkes not showin' up no more. We can't afford to have folks talk. Somebody'll hafta ride to town t'night and tell Jed Raines what happened."

A swift interchange of glances passed, but nobody volunteered for the mission. Preston hesitantly turned to Hatfield.

"Hatfield," he said, "your hoss looks purty fresh and ours has had a hard day. The boys is all 'bout tuckered out, too. You mind ridin' to town and tellin' the sheriff what happened?"

"Not a-tall," Hatfield replied instantly. He noted relief on the part of the others.

"Grab yourself a bite to eat while we put our cayuses up," said Preston. "C'mon, boys, these bronc's need some lookin' after 'fore they're bedded down. Hank, take Curly's feet fust, and we'll lay him in his bunk till the sheriff gets here. Leave them two hydrophobic skunks where they are."

Hatfield slipped the saddle from Goldy and let the sorrel roll.

"I'll give him a helpin' of oats while you eat," offered Hilton.

Half an hour later Jim Hatfield was riding swiftly toward Cuevas. The others were still busied in the barn with their horses. The concentration furrow was deep between the Ranger's black brows as the big sorrel *clicked* along the trail. He knew that Preston and his men had taken an undue amount of time to attend to the simple wants of the sturdy horses. The cayuses had been ridden hard, but they were in no distress. A quick rubdown was all any of them needed.

Plainly the Circle P owner and his old hands did not wish to enter the ranch house until the new man had left. It was unnatural, also, that they should send a man who had been in the employ of the ranch a scant twenty-four hours on such a mission as Hatfield was performing. It was obvious that they wished to get rid of him for the moment. Why?

That was what puzzled the Ranger, among other things. Where had Preston and his men been? From where had they ridden with such breakneck speed? It had been a long ride undoubtedly. He recalled what he had learned about the bloody triangle. His mind's eye ran over the portrayed route of the Cingaro Trail.

There were rumors, Lonnie Garret had said, that there was a way into Pardusco Cañon from the neighborhood of Cuevas. It was possible, admitting the existence of that outlet, for men to ride from the spot where Curly Wilkes had been shot to the Circle P ranch house by way of the Cingaro Trail. Jim's eyes narrowed at the thought. Preston and his men might possibly have been the dry-gulchers with Curly's duty that of leading the victim into a previously planned ambush. But if so, what was the motive behind the action?

It was long after midnight when he reached Cuevas, but the town was still going full blast. He shouldered his way to a bar and asked where he could locate the sheriff.

"His office is jest 'round the corner, two streets up," said the barkeep. "You won't find him there, though," he added as he poured the Ranger a drink. "He's out chasin' the jiggers what held up a stage and shot the driver and the guard. Yeah, they got a good haul . . . the payroll for the mines. It was bein' brought to the Cuevas bank from Crater . . . all in gold. The stage was held up 'bout five miles nawth of here jest 'fore dark by four mighty salty *hombres!*"

IX

"EYES OF DEATH"

The Ranger stood quietly sipping his drink as the bartender attended to the wants of another customer. He gazed straight into the mirror of the back-bar, but saw neither his own reflection nor those of the drinkers nearby. He was seeing four dusty, travel-stained men pulling their reeking horses to a halt in the Circle P ranch house yard.

He remembered noting that the rigs of Hilton and Kearns were equipped with saddlebags, something seldom included in the riding gear of cowboys with steady jobs on a comparatively small spread. He wondered with an intense curiosity what these two sets of bulging bags had contained.

For some minutes Hatfield stood, staring at his reflection. The man in the mirror stared back, lean of jaw, hard of mouth, eyes glinting coldly on either side of his high-bridged nose.

It was not exactly a handsome face that stared back at him. There was too much rugged man power in it for that. The thin-lipped mouth was a trifle too wide, the cheek bones too high, the brows too heavy and dark. The fine eyes redeemed the somewhat ominous features. They were large, slightly long, and set deeply beneath the dark brows. In color they were a peculiar shade of gray-green that now was chillingly cold.

They could be sunny, those level eyes, and then, when the thin lips quirked at the corners and the white, even teeth flashed beneath them, women, and men, found themselves strangely drawn to the tall man with the wide shoulders and slim, quiet hands. Children, dogs, and horses never had any fear of Jim Hatfield and imposed on him shamefully, something men never tried a second time and seldom once.

The bartender, a loquacious soul, came back to Hatfield and resumed his discussion of the robbery.

"None of the passengers could tell what they looked like?" Jim Hatfield asked after the drink juggler had finished his story.

"Nope. Two of them were masked and t'other two had blood or red paint smeared all over their faces till they looked like Injuns. Calculate the passengers were too scared to see anythin' straight anyhow. Bert or John might 'a' seen somethin', but they was both dead.

"Mebbe the sheriff'll git 'em. Stick 'round here if you wanna see him. He'll be shore to come here for a drink soon as he gits in . . . allus does. Here, have one on the house while you're waitin'."

Jim Hatfield took his drink to a nearby table and sat down to wait for the sheriff. The room was not so crowded now, for it was getting along toward morning. He ran his eyes over the scattering of men, drinking at the bar or gambling, and saw no one he knew.

Suddenly his glance centered on the swinging doors. A man was just coming through them whose face was familiar. A moment later he recognized *Don* Fernando Cartina. The ranch owner saw him at the same instant and came over to the table. He nodded a greeting, and sat down wearily.

"Tequila," he told the waiter who hurried up for his order.

Hatfield returned the nod, and his gaze ran over Cartina. The latter's hat and clothes were powdered with reddish dust. His face had a tired look, and there were dark circles under his eyes.

"Has the sheriff got back yet?" he asked. "I guess you've heard about the robbery?"

Hatfield nodded.

"The payroll for my mine was in that strongbox," he went on. "I don't stand to lose anything, of course. The money was still in charge of the bank, but it confuses things, and I had to come in to make arrangements. One of my men was in town, and he hustled right out to the ranch with the news, and my foreman and I rode straight to town at once. Just got here."

"Barkeep said the sheriff would be shore to stop here when he got in," Hatfield offered.

"I'll wait a bit," replied Cartina. "I've got to look up Darnel, the bank cashier, and see what he can do about the payroll. Have you landed a job yet?"

"Uhn-huh," Hatfield told him, "I'm workin' for the Circle P."

Don Fernando stared at him with slightly narrowed eyes. There was a coldness in his voice that had not been there before when he spoke.

"You evidently work fast. I can't help but feel, however, that it would have been better if you had signed up with some other spread."

"You can't be too choosey when you need a job," Hatfield replied.

"That's so," admitted *Don* Fernando. "Well, ride out to my place whenever you get time. You take the first trail to the north after you pass out of town heading east. Can't lose your way. It's a plain trail across the grassland all the way."

Hatfield's face did not change, but there was a slight glow in the depths of his level eyes.

"Grassland all the way?" the Ranger repeated the phrase questioningly. "Plain trail across it?"

"Yes," replied Cartina. "Easy to follow . . . ten mile ride."

For some time, then, they sat sipping their drinks and saying little.

"I'm waiting on my foreman," *Don* Fernando observed at length. "He went to put the horses away and see if the sheriff was in his office. I think a lot of Pierce Kimble," he added. "He saved my life once."

"That's apt to make you think sorta well of a feller," Hatfield admitted.

After another silence, *Don* Fernando remarked: "Here he comes now."

The Ranger glanced at the man who was walking across the room toward them. He was a tall man, fully as tall as

141

Hatfield but of slighter build. There was a slight stoop to his wide shoulders. His arms, abnormally long, hung loosely at his sides and woodenly straight. The thin-fingered hands reminded the Lone Wolf of spearheads.

Pierce Kimble's face was of a peculiar dead-white coloring, and his eyes looked like splotches of ink on its expressionless expanse, save for a crawling red flame in their depths. It was like slow fire under dirty ice.

His nose was thin and straight, his mouth a wide reptilian gash above a long cleft chin. He glided rather than walked across the floor, his gait something akin to the sideward slither of a coyote.

Don Fernando's foreman wore faded overalls, vest swinging open over a blue woolen shirt, cowboy boots slightly run over at the heels, and a broad-brimmed black Stetson from under which his lank black hair hung straight and stringy. Reddish dust powdered both clothes and hair. He paused at the table, his murky eyes questioning *Don* Fernando.

"Pierce, this is Hatfield, the fellow I was telling you about," introduced the ranch owner. "He signed up with the Circle P since I saw him last."

Pierce Kimble nodded, and shook hands. His palm had a clammy feel, but his fingers were like steel wires.

"So you're workin' for Brant Preston?" he remarked questioningly, his voice a soft burr.

"Uhn-huh," Hatfield replied. "He's got a nice spread."

"Yeah, a nice outfit," agreed Kimble. Looking the Ranger fully in the eyes, he smiled, a slow, creeping smile that writhed along his paper-thin red lips lifting them from his sharp, crooked and slightly yellow teeth, wrinkling his dead-colored cheeks, but never reaching his jet eyes. As that slow smile came and went, the Lone Wolf understood the feelings of the hard-bitten little Wes Crowley. He, too, felt as if something were walking across his grave.

The kind of grin you get from a rattlesnake when he loops up and looks at you with his tail buzzing, he told himself. *Only this jigger wouldn't do any buzzing. Hell, associating with him is pretty hefty pay even for having your life saved.*

"Sheriff ain't there," Kimble said, addressing himself to *Don* Fernando. "Who knows when he will be. I s'gest we go see Darnel and then hightail it for home. Damn' little sleep last night and none a-tall t'night. Darnel can 'tend to things, and there ain't nothin' the sheriff can do, even if he catches them jaspers, which he won't. That old fossil couldn't ketch his shadder with the sun shinin' in front of him!"

"Yes, I guess we might as well do that," admitted *Don* Fernando. "Take care of yourself, Hatfield. Drop in and see me."

"Mebbe I'll be droppin' in to see you and your outfit some time soon," observed Pierce Kimble. Again he looked Hatfield in the eyes and began his slow smile. Suddenly, however, his lips stiffened and his black gaze faltered. The eyes into which he stared had grown cold as frosted gun muzzles.

For a moment he tried to meet the Lone Wolf's icy glance, but something in that glance smashed his lids down as a physical blow. His spearhead hands raised slightly toward the black butts of the heavy guns swinging low against his stringy hips, then dropped. Without a word he turned and followed *Don* Fernando from the saloon.

For minutes Jim Hatfield sat staring after him, intense speculation in his steady eyes. The Lone Wolf never forgot a face, or any peculiar physical characteristic or action.

He's older, he mused, thinking of Pierce Kimble, *older*

and thinner, I think, but it's the same man. Five years since I saw him in Tombstone. So, here's where he landed! A dead man walking around. Calculate Wyatt Earp isn't such a good shot as he sets up to be. Hatfield's eyes flared wide, and he gazed into space. *And they both had red dust on their clothes!*

X

"NOT SO BAD"

The dawn sky was blushing pink as the cheek of a girl before Sheriff Jed Raines showed up. He was weary, sweat-stained, and reddish dust lay thickly in the folds of his rusty coat, but his big shoulders were square, and he held himself stiffly erect.

Hatfield liked the grim old face with its frosty gray eyes and its bristling mustache. Behind him shambled his stoop-shouldered, gawky deputy whose soft brown eyes and mild voice had been the undoing of more than one badman not blessed with keenness of perception.

The Ranger walked over to meet the sheriff. Raines looked at him questioningly.

"I'd like to have a word with you, Sheriff, if you aren't too tired," Hatfield requested deferentially.

Old Jed Raines bristled. "Who the hell said I was tired?" he growled. His chill glance ran over the Ranger's tall form. "Appears to me you mightily resemble the feller that picked up the ruckus in Casuse's *cantina* t'other night," he remarked.

Hatfield noticed the deputy sidle casually past him and bit back a grin with difficulty.

"Uhn-huh," he admitted, "wouldn't be surprised if I do

look sort of like that fellow."

The sheriff's jaw dropped slightly. Jim Hatfield went on before he had time to speak: "You see, Sheriff, I'm working for Brant Preston of the Circle P."

Jed Raines's jaw snapped back tightly; his eyes glowed angrily.

"There was a little trouble out there yesterday," Hatfield continued quickly. "It was like this. . . ." Tersely he outlined the happenings at the Circle P. "Preston calculated you ought to know about it. He thought mebbe you might want to investigate," he finished.

"Yeah, I calculate I will," grunted the sheriff. "And I calculate I'll wanna investigate you a bit, too, young feller."

His glance was over the Ranger's shoulder as he spoke, and Hatfield was not in the least surprised to feel a cold circle jammed against his neck.

Still struggling with the grin, he raised his hands to the level of his shoulder before the deputy could even drawl his mild order to elevate.

"You're showin' sense, anyhow," grunted Raines, relieving Hatfield of his hardware. "All right, out the front door, and don't try nothin' funny. You're purty lanky, but this ol' shootin' iron of mine is a damn' sight huskier. Jest take it easy and stay healthy."

The big room was in an uproar, but a glance from the sheriff's cold eyes quelled the tumult to a hum. Nobody followed them through the swinging doors.

In front of the sheriff's office, which was the front room of the little jail, the deputy held the prisoner until Jed Raines got a light going. Then he marched Ranger Jim Hatfield into the office.

Here Raines searched him thoroughly, the deputy lounging easily by the door. He felt under the Ranger's arms for shoulder holsters and at the back of his neck for a possible knife. He was patting the front of his shirt when he felt something hard under the gray flannel.

The sheriff jerked a button open and fumbled inside the shirt. It took him some time to get the little secret pocket open. Hatfield grinned with whole-hearted amusement as the sheriff's fingers probed the pocket and drew forth what it contained. As he stared at the object, the old officer's jaw sagged, his eyes goggled.

"Well, I'll be eternally damned!" he swore with fervor.

Hipless Harley, the deputy, peered over Hatfield's shoulder, and his own jaw dropped, as he saw on the sheriff's horny palm a small silver star on a silver circle.

"Good gosh-all-hemlock, Sheriff! A *Ranger!*"

Sheriff Raines swore again, an exultant note in his voice this time. "So you fellers did get here, after all!" he exclaimed. "I never expected it. I told Fernando Cartina the day I was wishin' for a troop that there waren't a chance in the world to get one right now, the shape things is in over the state. He insisted I write a letter anyhow, that it couldn't do no harm, and it would be a good thing to have it on file. Said he'd write one, too. Here, take these hawglegs of yours back, and here's your star. When'll the rest of your troop be along?"

"Oh, about the Thirty-First of February," Hatfield replied.

"Thirty-Fust of Feb'rary?" rejoined the sheriff. "Hell, there ain't no Thirty-Fust of Feb'rary!"

"Exactly!" The Ranger's green eyes smiled down at him, and the corners of his wide mouth quirked up as he drawled the single word across a white-toothed grin.

Sheriff Raines's jaw dropped, then he got the Ranger's meaning, and started to swear again. Hipless Harley, in the meantime, had been taking in the Lone Wolf's lean, muscular body, hard, bronzed jaw, and level eyes. His mild drawl stopped the sheriff's angry profanity.

"Puhsonally, and ev'thin considered," said Harley, "I calculate we ain't done so bad!"

"Now what's the next move?" inquired Sheriff Raines as he, the deputy, and the erstwhile prisoner sat smoking behind drawn shades.

"First thing," said the Ranger, "is to point out to me the cleanest bunk of that jailhouse of yours and let me garner a little shut-eye. It's been quite a spell since I laid my weary head down low enough to stop the blood running to my feet. Then you can lock the door on me. Here, take my hardware first."

He drew his guns and handed them to the sheriff.

"What the hell?" exploded Raines. "You ain't under arrest!"

"Nope," Hatfield told him soberly, "but I'd better be. Would look sort of funny if I weren't, the way you larruped me outta that saloon after hearin' what I had to say. I don't hanker to have folks around hereabouts getting suspicious about me . . . not till I have a better idea who's who and who isn't. My best bet is to keep under cover for a while."

"Calculate you're right 'bout that," admitted Raines. "Then what?"

The Lone Wolf replied instantly, his voice crisp with the unconscious authority of a man accustomed to having his orders obeyed without question.

"This afternoon," he told Jed Raines, "you and Harley and a couple more deputies ride out to the Circle P. Preston and his outfit'll be expectin' you. Bring in the bodies, and bring in the Circle P outfit and lock 'em up. It won't hurt 'em to spend a night behind the bars. Get a coroner's jury together and have it sit tomorrow. No jury'll hold me or Preston or any of the rest of 'em after we tell our story, but it'll look good. It'll tie me up definitely with the Circle P outfit, and that's what I want. I calculate that's the last place folks hereabouts would expect to find a Ranger, and it'll be a good cover for me while I work on the rustlings and killings around here."

"I'll say so," grunted the sheriff. "They 'bout as soon expect to find one of them Circle P hellions in church. I'll tend to it. Ol' Doc Beard is the coroner, and Doc'll handle things like I tell him to. We'll go through with ev'thin' law-'bidin' and reg'lar. I'll have Doc hand out one of them little the jury says you ain't guilty, but don't do it ag'in talks of his'n. That oughta help. *Don* Fernando'll chuckle when he hears 'bout all this."

"*Don't* do any talking just yet to anybody about what went on here tonight," Hatfield counseled. "The best-intentioned folks in the world make slips sometimes. People that don't know things can't talk at the wrong time."

"That makes sense," agreed the sheriff. "I can keep my mouth shut, and Harley is too damn' lazy to talk. We'll jest let things ride as they is."

"Then that's settled," Hatfield said, rising to his feet and stretching his long arms until the sinews cracked. "It isn't hard to get to *Don* Fernando's spread, is it, in case I should want to get there?"

"Nope," replied the sheriff. "Plain trail across the grassland all the way. Ten miles of easy ridin'."

"Good rangeland all the way? Must be a mighty fine spread."

"It is," nodded the sheriff. "Curly mesquite and needle grass all the way from here to the F Bar C ranch house, and then on nawth till you hit that strip of desert jest before you come to the hills. Best range in this section. Not an acre of desert. Anythin' else on your mind?" he asked.

"Yeah," the Ranger replied. "I want paper and pen and ink."

His request being granted, Hatfield sat at the sheriff's desk and wrote three letters. One was addressed to Captain Bill McDowell of the Rangers. Another went to the sheriff at Tombstone, Arizona, and the third to the warden of the penitentiary in Arizona.

"I'm havin' the answers come addressed to you," he told Sheriff Raines. "Hold 'em for me, and get word to me if you can, *pronto*. Another thing, what kind of a jigger is the bank cashier, Darnel, I believe Cartina said his name is? I want to have a talk with him pretty soon."

"Darnel's all right," said the sheriff. "You can trust him to keep his mouth shut. What you want to talk to him for?" he added curiously.

"One way to find out what folks are doing is to find out how they spend their money," Hatfield told him. "There's more to these killings and torturings than appears on the surface. Whoever is doin' it is doin' it because they want to put the fear of God in somebody. From what you say, every jigger that's been tortured has been a *peón* from the river villages. Somebody wants to get the *peónes* scared proper. Scare 'em enough and you can make 'em do anythin' and, what's more, keep quiet about it. Looks like the jigger that wants something done is the gent they call El Hombre. Question is . . . what does he want? I've got a notion, but there isn't much so far to tie it up with. Find out what's back of it all, and finding El Hombre won't be so hard."

The sheriff snorted. "Sounds sorta like foolishness to me," he grumbled, "but you can do what you like."

"By the way," the Ranger added, "just where did *Don* Fernando Cartina come from?"

"Allus lived here," replied the sheriff. "Grandfather was born t'other side the river . . . pure Spanish blood. Fernando's mother was from Arizona . . . she waren't Mexican. Were a widow, I understand, 'fore she married Fernando Cartina's dad. Them and Fernando spent lots of time in Arizona 'fore she died . . . her folks lived there. Fine people, from what I allus heerd."

Jim Hatfield nodded. "Let me have those letters back a minute," he said. "Just recollect I forgot something."

He ripped one open, added a few more words, and re-sealed it in a fresh envelope.

Ten minutes later the Lone Wolf was asleep on a hard little bunk. As he slept, four men sat around a table in a big ranch house room and talked in low tones. The single lamp was turned low, and their faces were but whitish blurs in the shadows.

"I tell you I know what I'm talkin' 'bout!" one declared fiercely. "I never seed him but onct, and I didn't get much of a look then, but I did see his eyes, and I never forgot them eyes and never will. You can't forget 'em, once you look inter 'em when he means business.

"Ain't no wonder he's raised hell ever since he hit this section. He's done for five men already, and him and that damn' hoss of his'n has crippled four more. Three times we tried for him and didn't get him.

"Range tramp hell! That jasper ain't no wanderin' cowpoke lookin' for work from t'other side of the hills. That plumb pizen gent is a Ranger, that's what he is, and I'm tellin' you right now he's wus'n that. *He's* the *Lone Wolf!*"

There was an uneasy shifting of feet at this statement.

"Question is," continued the speaker, "what we gonna do?"

"Only one thing to do," said the man who sat at the head of the table. He drew his hand across his throat in a significant gesture.

"Uhn-huh," grumbled the other, "the whole business is gonna be hell a-tootin' if that sidewinder is left loose and fangin'. Yeah, jest one thing to do, but, gents, I'm tellin' you, it's gonna be *some chore!*"

Hatfield slept comfortably most of the day. He awoke hungry and was glad when he heard keys rattling against the outer door. A little later the entire Circle P outfit was ushered in, including Hang Soon, the cook.

Brant Preston and his cowpunchers were fighting mad and spoke their opinion of the sheriff in no uncertain terms. Hang Soon rolled apprehensive slant eyes and said things that would have tangled up a sidewinder with the colic. Hatfield vociferously demanded something to eat.

Food was brought in due time, surprisingly good and a surprisingly large amount of it. After getting on the outside of it, the prisoners were in a better temper.

"Just take it easy," the Ranger counseled the others. "The jury won't hold us any longer than it takes to hear our stories. It'll just be a matter of form."

"It's that damn' Jed Raines!" growled Preston. "He's got it in for me proper. He won't never be satisfied till he gets me shot or hung."

"If you didn't try to shine up to that niece of his'n, and if you and her pa hadn't . . . ," began the irascible little Crowley.

Preston turned furious blue eyes on him. "Shet your damn' mouth!" he blazed. "You're allus talkin' outta turn!"

Crowley subsided, muttering sullenly to himself. Jim Hatfield would have given much to have had him finish his interrupted statement.

Old Doc Beard opened court in Flintlock Finnegan's saloon shortly after midday. The news had got about, and the big room was crowded. Jim Hatfield saw *Don* Fernando Cartina, who nodded to him cordially. He saw nothing of *Don* Fernando's evil-appearing foreman, Pierce Kimble. Lonnie Garret was there, and she stared at him coldly.

Guess the little lady doesn't approve of the company I'm keeping, Hatfield told himself with a rueful grin.

Last in the line of prisoners was Hang Soon, and, as he entered, an indignant feminine voice rent the air.

"Arragh!" the woman exclaimed, "and there's the yaller haythen what bedeviled me poor husband and led him in evil ways. Just let me get me grippers on his skinny neck, and they won't be afther needin' a rope!"

Hang Soon gave a despairing squeak and tried to bolt, but was stopped by Hipless Harley.

"Me go back jail," chattered Hang. "Me throw 'way with key! That wife without boss! Me wanna be allee same China."

"You'll get a good start in that d'rection if you don't stop tryin' to get past me," Harley told him grimly. "You'll get down thataway three, four feet, anyhow."

"Two feet plenty, if get chance to use um," wailed Hang.

"Order in the court!" bawled old Doc Beard, his white whiskers bristling. "I'm runnin' this shindig, and, when I need any assistance, I'll ask for it!"

Doc Beard banged on the table with an ancient horse pistol with a muzzle the size of a nail keg. The old cannon was at full cock, and several gentlemen hurriedly vacated front seats.

The jury was sworn in, and the trial proceeded swiftly. After Hank Hilton had told the last story, old Doc glared venomously at the prisoners and addressed the jury.

"These fellows stick together," he said, "and we haven't got a way to contradict 'em. Also, so far as we can find out, there wasn't anybody plugged but one of their own gang and two mighty mean-lookin' Mexicans, so, gents, I calculate the only thing we can do is turn 'em loose till next time.

"Mebbe by then the law of averages and general cussedness will thin 'em out some more. Finnegan, you will serve the court and the jury free drinks. The prisoners and the spectators'll pay for their own."

Crowley, Hilton, and Kearns began celebrating their release with some cronies at one end of the bar. Hatfield cast about in search of Preston, but could not find him. Shortly he headed for the livery stable to see if Goldy was all right. He was in the sorrel's stall when a man and a girl paused in the doorway of the stable. The Ranger recognized Brant Preston and Lonnie Garret. They were conversing in low tone.

"Lonnie, I tell you it waren't my fault," Preston was saying, his voice pleading. "I tried to get him out, but there waren't a chance. The only thing for me to do was cut and run for it. I calculated on goin' back for him, but I never could get a chanct. They was after me ev'ry step to the border. You know I'm tellin' you the truth. I. . . ."

"All I know," the girl interrupted fiercely, "is that you got away yourself and left Dad to rot in that Mexican jail. He's been there for months now. Maybe he's dead." Her voice choked on a sob. "I never want to see your face again," she declared. "Why shouldn't I believe the things

153

they say about you? Why shouldn't I believe it is you that's stealing cattle and butchering Mexicans? Uncle Jed says it's you, even if he can't prove it."

"Jed Raines . . . ," Preston began angrily, but his voice instantly grew gentle again. "After all, he's your dead mother's brother, so I ain't sayin' anythin'," he finished.

"And I thought that tall, good-looking man who rode with me the other night was different!" exclaimed the girl. "Now I learn he was one of your outfit all the time. The way he pulled the wool over my eyes when I caught him branding my calf! I wish I'd aimed at him instead of his fire!"

And I'm shore glad you didn't, Hatfield said to himself as he stood in the shadow of Goldy's stall. *Maybe it isn't nice to listen, but this is shore getting interesting. Looks like* Señor *Preston has been mixed up in things aplenty. Pity such a nice little gal's dad was in the mess, too.*

He heard the girl's riding skirt *swish* into a neighboring stall. A moment later she led forth a sturdy little pinto and mounted with lithe grace.

"I tell you I never want to see your face again!" she flared at Brant Preston as she rode away. Preston stared after her a moment, and then walked across the street. In the semi-darkness of the stall, Jim Hatfield chuckled.

" 'Most every gent has a handle you can grab him and hold him by, if you just know what it is," he told the golden horse. "Yeah, I calculate that little redhead is the handle that's gonna help me get a hold of the big skookum he-wolf of the bunch that's raisin' all the hell in this district."

XI

"INTO THE SPIDER'S WEB"

Hatfield waited until Preston had turned the corner, then he, too, left the stable. He could hear the proprietor, an old broken-down wrangler, stumping about the little room partitioned off in a corner of the hayloft and knew that he had neither seen nor heard what had gone on in the doorway.

The Ranger reached the corner just in time to see Lonnie and *Don* Fernando Cartina riding out of town together. He went back to Flintlock Finnegan's saloon, his black brows drawn together slightly and his green eyes thoughtful. He found Brant Preston seated morosely at a table, a bottle and glass beside him. The ranch owner's greeting was barely civil, but Hatfield dropped into a vacant chair on the opposite side of the table. There were men at the bar, including Hank Hilton, Wes Crowley, and Tart Kearns, now well on the road to a royal drunk, but the nearby tables were unoccupied. The Ranger put his elbows on the table and stared across at Preston.

"Preston," Hatfield's voice was a soft drawl, "just where is that calaboose you left Miss Garret's dad in?"

Brant Preston's head jerked up, and his blue eyes were black with anger. "So you was listenin'! Why, damn you. . . ."

The Lone Wolf's quiet voice stemmed the tirade before it got under way. "I couldn't keep from hearin'," he said. "I was in the stall with my horse, and I didn't calculate it would help matters any by me walking out in the middle of your powwow. Now, tighten up on your rope a minute till

155

I'm finished. I'm not asking questions that aren't any of my business just to be curious. I happen to know something of Mexican jails, and, as I recollect, Miss Garret said her pa had been in one of 'em for months. If he stays there much longer, there won't be any use of him comin' out, except to bust up a dull day for the buzzards. You ought to know that, seein' as you say you've looked at the outside from one yourself."

Preston's eyes flickered slightly, and he swallowed, as if savoring an unpleasant memory. "Yeah, I was there, too," he admitted, "though not for long. I'll tell you how it all happened. . . ."

He cleared his throat and began talking slowly, apparently choosing his words with care. Jim Hatfield envisioned a table in a Cuevas saloon, around which sat a half dozen or so men. Preston was there, and *Don* Fernando Cartina. There was also Tom Garret, Lonnie's father, Craig Doyle, who owned the K8, and several cowboys.

"I'm sick and tired of the whole damn' bus'ness," Garret was swearing. "I lost 'nother herd this week. Few more raids and I won't have 'nough beef on my spread to make a sandwich."

Don Fernando nodded his handsome head. "We're all catching it," he agreed. "The question is . . . what are we going to do?"

"I know what I'm gonna do!" Garret declared grimly.

"What's that, Tom?" asked Craig Doyle.

Garret leaned across the table and spoke impressively. "I'm gonna get my steers back, that's what," he rumbled. "How? You jest listen. Ev'body knows where them beefs go when they cross the river . . . they goes to Tijerna, Juan Cheno's town."

"Yeah," agreed Preston, "they do. That's why we can't

do anythin' 'bout it. Cheno is a reg'lar king down thataway. Even old Pres'dent Díaz can't do anythin' with him. Díaz is scairt of him . . . scairt Cheno may start a rev'lution or somethin'. Cheno ain't got no eddication, can't read or write, but he shore has got brains of a sort."

"Brains of a wide-looper!" growled Garret. "Well, gents, I'm gonna tie a knot in *Señor* Cheno's rope. I'm gonna ride right down to his El Aguila Ranch, cut me out a herd, and bring 'em back 'crost the river. You fellers with me?"

For a moment there was stunned silence. Then young Craig Doyle let out a whoop.

"I'm with you, Tom!" he declared. "If Cheno can run 'em from this side, we can run 'em from his. You in on it, Brant?"

For a moment Preston's face was uncertain. Garret leaned forward, boring the younger man with his hot eyes.

"You'll play hell ever gettin' married, the way your cattle is disappearin'," he remarked.

Preston flushed, his lips tightened. "All right," he replied quickly. "I'll go you, Tom. I can take the chanct, if you can."

Don Fernando Cartina leaned forward and spoke earnestly. "You are all mad," he declared. "You are attempting the impossible. Cheno knows every move made along the border. If an armed force rides toward El Aguila, he will be notified. You will just end by getting killed."

"We're takin' that chanct," Garret replied grimly. "I don't blame you for not j'inin with us. Your prop'ty is chiefly mines. Cattle is jest a side issue with you, but it's the hull works with the rest of us."

Two nights later Preston, Garret, Craig Doyle, and five cowpunchers crossed the shallow river and rode south. All night they rode and, when daylight came, holed up in a burr oak grove and slept. That night, when the moon flooded the rangeland with ghostly silver, they rode swiftly south again.

El Aguila, Cheno's vast ranch, was as large as some kingdoms. Cheno, bloated, sinister, spider-like, ruled it as a king or a feudal baron. In Tijerna, his headquarters, he had a small army of hard-riding, hard-shooting *vaqueros*. Another army was scattered over his many thousands of acres. Not even the grim old tyrant of Mexico City could suppress him. Díaz hated Cheno, and feared him. He raided across the river and defied the Texas authorities to do anything about it.

Cattle by the thousand grazed on El Aguila. Tom Garret and his companions approached one of the vast, untended herds. They cut out as many as they could drive swiftly and turned their heads north.

"Easy!" exulted Garret. "Didn't I tell you we could do it?"

His men scattered about the herd, urging it on. On either side brooded dark hills, mysterious in the moonlight. The valley through which they were passing narrowed.

From those silent hills suddenly burst a storm blast of death. Rifles spurted red from the shelter of rock and tree trunk. Six-guns rattled as Cheno's yelling *vaqueros* swept down upon the doomed band.

Craig Doyle died at the first volley. Three of the cowboys died, also. The two others and Garret went down fighting, the two 'punchers riddled with bullets, Garret with a creased skull. A rope sailed through the air and settled over Brant Preston's shoulders.

In a moment he was helpless, bound by turn on turn of rawhide. He and Garret were thrown across horses. Their captors headed for Tijerna.

Cheno, the merciless, grinned at them and licked his thick lips.

"You will remain as my guests, *caballeros,*" he purred. "For long you will remain."

He waved a fat hand, and the prisoners were hustled away and thrown in the filthy little calaboose that crouched on the banks of a sluggish creek that skirted Cheno's town. Garret was weak and sick, his head badly gashed. Preston was unhurt. During the time that Garret spent in jail, he regained some measure of his strength. They plotted escape.

Hour after hour Preston whittled and shaped a piece of wood with a knife he had managed to smuggle in. One evening when the slovenly jailer shoved their scanty meal through the bars, he looked up and stared into the black muzzle of what appeared to be a serviceable gun.

"Open that damn' door," Preston's cold voice bit at him, "or have your brains spattered over the wall!"

Gasping, trembling, the jailer obeyed. The two prisoners slipped out, bound and gagged the jailer, and threw him into the cell. Preston tossed aside the wooden gun he had whittled out and replaced it with the jailer's big Smith & Wesson. Then they crept through the shadows toward a stable in which were housed the mounts of some of Cheno's soldiers.

"*¿Quién es?*" asked the wrangler as they loomed in the dark doorway. Garret leaped like a panther and smashed him between the eyes with his fist. Working with frantic speed, they saddled two horses, mounted, and rode through the low doorway, straight into a troop of Cheno's *vaqueros.*

Bending low in the saddle, lashing his horse, Preston burst through their ranks before the surprised Mexicans knew what was going on. Close behind him thundered

Garret. Guns *boomed* behind them. The *vaqueros* gave chase.

Preston, on the better horse, forged ahead. Suddenly he heard a yell, then a howl of triumph. Garret's horse was down, and Garret lay senseless beside him in the dust. For a moment Preston hesitated, pulling his broncho to a sliding halt, but before he could turn, the *vaqueros* were swarming about Garret. Preston whirled his mount and hightailed for the border.

"Mebbe I'd oughta gone back for him, anyhow, and died there," Preston concluded, staring into the Ranger's face, "but right then I couldn't figger it would do either of us any good. I calculated, if I could get 'crost the river, I might be able to do Tom some good from this side. I've tried damn' hard, but so far I ain't been able to accomplish anythin'. I did find out he was still alive and in jail."

"Yeah, Cheno is the sort that knows it's tougher bein' shut up in that hell hole than bein' dead." Hatfield nodded.

"I had to tell Lonnie 'bout it," Preston went on. "She sorta held it 'gainst me, and folks here'bouts didn't think any too well of the hull bus'ness. They seem to figger we jest went on a wide-loopin' trip. What bothers me most is to think of Garret there in that damn' jail."

Jim Hatfield was evolving a plan. He leaned forward, and his level green gaze beat against Preston's face.

"Why leave him there?" he asked softly.

Preston stared at Hatfield as if suspecting that he had suddenly lost his mind. "How in hell am I gonna keep from leavin' him there?" he demanded.

Hatfield's steady eyes did not leave the other's face. "You can keep from it by getting him out and bringing him home," he said.

Preston swore viciously. "You tryin' to be funny?" he

160

asked. "Cheno's got five hundred men in that damn' town of his and five hundred more scattered 'round his spreads. How in hell am I gonna buck up 'gainst a young army?"

The Lone Wolf's voice snapped at him like a pistol crack. "By using what you have got . . . brains! If you've got sand to go along with them!"

Preston's face turned livid, and his eyes blazed blue fire. He swallowed convulsively and steadied his voice with an effort. The anger died out as he stared at the Ranger's impassive face. "Feller," he said at last, "I'm listenin'. What you got to s'gest?"

Jim Hatfield hauled the makings from his pocket and rolled a cigarette with the slim fingers of one hand before replying.

"I know Cheno's got a little army down there," he admitted, "and I know we don't have the men to go up against him, but a snake can crawl in a hole that a grizzly can't . . . and he can do a hell of a lotta damage after he gets through.

"Now if about three fellows . . . say you and me and that little jigger, Crowley . . . were to slip down there looking like Mexicans and do a little snoopin' around, mebbe we could put one over on *Señor* Cheno. I figure it's worth trying, anyhow."

Preston digested the Ranger's remark. "All you need is a dirty blanket and a sombrero to make Crowley look like a greaser," he admitted, "and me, I wouldn't have much trouble getting by either by addin' a little grease and some velvet pants, but you, feller, there ain't no makin' a Mexican outta you."

"Nope," Hatfield agreed, "but I know how to make up to pass for an Indian. I've done it before. All I need is some buckskin pants and a shirt and a chance to use a kettle in the ranch house kitchen."

Brant Preston's face became animated. "Feller," he declared, "I'm with you. Chances are it'll jest end up by all three of us bein' cashed in or keepin' old Tom company, but I'm with you. I can answer for Crowley, too. That little hell-raiser is in for anythin' what promises a fight."

Jim stood up, towering over the rancher. "All right," he said, his voice ringing and decisive. "We'll hunt up Crowley. Don't tell him what you're figuring on doin' till you get him to the ranch. Don't tell anybody. I mean *nobody a-tall!* You can leave word at the ranch for the other boys that you're on a little trip and for them to look after the spread till you get back. All's needed is one little slip, one word in the wrong place from somebody, and we'll all three stay in *Méjico.* So long as nobody but us three knows we're down there, I calculate we got a reasonable chance."

Crowley was a good deal more than half drunk, but Preston managed to haul him away from Flintlock's bar and get him headed for the ranch. Jim Hatfield rode with them. Several times in the course of the ride he dismounted to gather a handful of berries, a few leaves, or a root or two from a soft hillside. These he carefully wrapped in a handkerchief and carried along with him. At the ranch house kitchen the whole mess went into a small iron pot and simmered over a slow fire, much to the disgust of Hang Soon.

"Smell like dead cow inside buzzard's belly," declared the Chinaman. "Me hang nose on line with clothes pin . . . allee same shut tight on outside."

The Ranger grinned, and set the pot aside to cool. When he could bear the touch of it, he smeared the thick liquid over his face, neck, hands, and forearms. The result was startling. With his skin now stained to a reddish bronze, his hawk nose, high cheek bones, and straight black hair, the resemblance to a Plains Indian would have fooled a Blackfoot or a Sioux. A suit of frayed buckskin that he had managed to pick up in a Cuevas store made the disguise complete.

"Me gonna take hair off and put um in pocket," declared Hang. "No want um hang on belt."

"Don't worry, Hang, you ain't gonna git scalped," chuckled a villainous-looking little "Mexican" who lounged in the door, a cornhusk cigarette drooping from his lower lip.

"This one look bad. Mist' Crowley, you look worse," declared Hang. "Mist' Preston look bad from worse of all!"

Crowley and Preston *were* a forbidding pair, Hatfield was forced to admit. His black brows drew together as he gazed at the latter, garbed in Mexican attire, sombrero pulled low over his smoldering eyes. Once again Jim recalled a vision of a dark, sinister face rushing toward him out of the night.

The bonfire stars of Texas were burning golden over their heads, the blue dust of the dusk deepening to black velvet about them when the three ominous figures crossed the murmuring flood of the Río Grande and rode into that brooding, mysterious land beyond. Far to the south, sitting like a bloated spider in its web, Cheno, the merciless, awaited their coming.

XII

"HELL AND HIGH WATER"

It was mid-afternoon, with Tijerna lying sun-drenched and shiftless at the foot of a towering mountain whose crest of naked rock seemed to rake the brassy-blue sky. Forests of scrub oak and piñon pine, like cool green and blue shadows, clothed the sides and shoulders of the old giant, but the needle spire that fanged up like a blackened tooth in a rotting jawbone was undraped save for the saffron waves of light that streamed about it.

As Jim Hatfield and his two companions rode into Tijerna, those waves were turning from saffron to rose, with little trickles of crimson spilling down the grooved crags like pulses of slow blood. Tijerna itself, with the straggle of adobes sprawling toward the mountains, its *cantinas,* gambling hells, and pleasure palaces, was splashed with molten gold. Over everything was a powdering of yellow dust.

Even the serapes and sombreros of the loungers about the plaza were thick with it. Dogs wallowed in it, as well as hogs and naked children. Scrawny chickens flapped up small clouds with indolent wings as they burrowed out little hollows. The hoofs of the newcomers' horses plumped in it with soft little *chucks.* Goldy sneezed and rolled his eyes in disgust.

Hatfield, his red-bronze face devoid of expression, thought that never before had he encountered such vicious shiftlessness as Cheno's town evinced. Beady eyes glinted sideward to watch their progress along the street. No word was said. The dark faces of the loungers told nothing of what was going on in their furtive minds, but the Ranger could sense an air of tense calculation and dangerous curiosity.

As they rode along, Hatfield wondered if those snaky eyes could penetrate their disguises. If such were the case, he knew that they had not one chance in a thousand of getting out of the town alive. Every man he saw was armed, and he knew that every man in the town was one of Cheno's bandit soldiers and, despite an appearance of utter indolence, was a vicious, alert fighter who knew nothing of either fear or mercy.

These men were one with the three hard-faced Yaqui-Mexicans he had encountered on the banks of the little stream as he rode to Cuevas. They were kin, also, to the men who had tried so desperately to murder him in the Cuevas saloon and, later, in the Circle P bunkhouse.

Jim Hatfield's eyes narrowed slightly at the realization. In the depths of his mind, mistily as yet, began to breed an idea—the first concrete thing amid the gropings for the elusive motive behind the seemingly senseless killings and torturings that had terrorized the bloody triangle north of the Río Grande.

"El Hombre," he muttered under his breath. "El Hombre . . . Juan Cheno! Wonder if the two do tie up. If they do . . . if they're the same! Hell. . . ."

His black brows drew together as he envisioned what it would mean to the border country if Cheno, the bandit, the revolutionary, really was the dread and mysterious El Hombre, the very mention of whom caused the *peónes* of the river villages to blanch and shiver.

We'll figure on that later, he decided as they drew up in front of a tawdry *mesón*. This tavern was the kind that catered to trade such as he and his ragged and dirty companions represented.

They entered the inn, conversing glumly in liquidly slurred Spanish, asked food for themselves and provender for their horses. The innkeeper demanded payment in advance, and Hatfield handed out the required amount in small silver coins.

The innkeeper, who acted as his own wrangler, eyed the big sorrel greedily, turned, and found the cold eyes of the Indian owner of the animal staring down into his face. The Indian said nothing, only he drew from somewhere, the innkeeper never knew where, an enormous knife and ran a bronzed fingertip along the razor-sharp edge, gazing hungrily at the man's shock of greasy black hair the while. The other turned a dirty gray under the dirt that encrusted his swarthy face.

"*Señor,* your *caballo* will receive such care as I would lavish on my eldest son, had I a son," he assured. "Fear not, he will be at your call, instantly and at all times."

The Indian said nothing. He put the knife away with evident reluctance and stalked into the eating room of the inn with the gait of a mountain lion.

"*Madre de Dios,*" breathed the innkeeper as he shuffled toward the stable.

Preston and Crowley, who had witnessed the bit of byplay, were hard put to hide the grins that twitched their lips.

"I got a hunch we ain't gonna be bothered by hoss thieves," breathed the latter.

They ate hungrily of a stew of black beans and meat, fiery with ground red peppers, and flat tortilla biscuits, washing it down with *pulque.* The Mexican beer, brewed from cactus juice, was heady and good. The food, although coarse, was also good and well-prepared.

"We're bein' watched damned close," Hatfield told his companions between mouthfuls. "They're a suspicious lot here . . . calculate they got plenty reason to be. I got a hunch somebody'll be driftin' to sound us out before long. Cheno doesn't let strangers ride into his town without finding out something about them. Brant, you do the talking."

They had just ordered another drink when a slim young Mexican in velvet jacket and pantaloons sauntered through the room and, with a glance around the room, strolled over to their table.

"*Perdona mi curiosidad, caballeros,*" he said courteously, "but I could not but notice the wonderful *caballo* ridden by the tall *señor*. I am a lover of fine horses, and I hope you will not consider it an affront when I say that I would greatly like to purchase the animal. It is for sale, perhaps, if the price is right, *sí?*"

Hatfield vigorously shook his head but said nothing.

Preston took up the conversation in Spanish. "The chief here thinks greatly of his horse," he explained. "Men died when he acquired it."

The other raised his delicate eyebrows. "*Sí,* I understand," he replied, instantly accepting the implication that the horse was stolen. "You have ridden far?" he asked.

"From the river, and beyond," replied Preston.

Again the other nodded. The implication there was that the horse, doubtless the others, also, were stolen from a Texas ranch.

"You will drink with us, *señor?*" invited Preston. This time he paid for the drinks with a gold piece, which did not escape the guest's keen eyes, or the glint of other gold in Preston's palm. He was beginning to understand better why these three had ridden from beyond the river.

"You will remain in our town for some days?" the Mexican asked.

"Perhaps," replied Preston. "*¿Quién sabe?*" with a shrug. A moment later he asked, with elaborate casualness, a question that on the surface seemed irrelevant. "The *Rurales,*" Preston queried, "they come here often?" He knew very well that El Presidente's mounted police never visited Cheno's town, or rode over his millions of acres.

The other knew very well that he knew it and grinned his appreciation. His voice was cordial and comradely when he replied. "No one in the town of *el gran general* need fear the

Rurales," he stated, voicing the title given Cheno by his followers.

Preston returned the grin. Crowley grinned, also, and Hatfield gave vent to a guttural grunt that might have signified pleasure or any other emotion. After another drink, the stranger bade them a courteous—*"Buenos días."*—and left the room.

"Well, that's that," said the Ranger. "He's got us down as a gang of raiders with the border too hot to hold us. Another day or two and chances are we'll get an invite to join Cheno's army. Now the first thing is to get in touch with Garret. Crowley, I calculate that'll be your chore. You ought to be able to mix best with the rooster fighters and gamblers and such. He's gotta know what we're gonna do before we start anything. Now here's what I've got in mind. . . ."

He spoke rapidly for some minutes, and, as he went on, Crowley's little eyes snapped, and he chuckled with pleasure.

"Feller, you're good," he declared. "I been wonderin' all 'long how in hell we was gonna bust open that jail 'thout dynamite or somethin'. If that scheme don't work, I'm a sheepherder. Don't worry, I'll get word to ol' Garret. He'll be ready and waitin'."

It took Crowley less than twenty-four hours to make good his word, slip into the jail, and have a word with Garret.

"One of the fellers I been gamblin' with had a bunky what sliced another hellion over a cockfight," he explained to Hatfield. "Cheno had him locked up a while to cool off. Him and Garret is the only pris'ners in the jail right now. They ain't locked in cells, day or night. Ain't no cells in the damn' hawg waller, that's why . . . jest one big room with a door openin' inter another room where the jailer sleeps.

"The one winder, barred good and strong, looks over the creek what runs in back of the jail, jest as you figgered. The back of the jail is set on high posts, 'cause the crick gets up a bit when it rains hard. Water is washin' against them posts right now. I told Garret to be ready t'night."

"Time for us to move, then," the Ranger told the others.

An hour later they were riding south out of the town. The inhabitants watched them depart with expressionless, beady eyes, but offered no objection. Before sundown they were among the lonely hills. They made camp in a little clearing, cooked some food, and allowed the horses to graze and roll. When twilight spread its golden-purple mantle across the rolling rangeland, they saddled up and headed back for Tijerna, letting the horses take it easy.

It was past midnight when they pulled up on the far bank of the shallow creek, directly opposite the little jail. Preston led a spare horse they had managed to cut out of a string grazing near a lonely ranch house, a few miles south of Tijerna.

Leaving Crowley to hold the horses, Hatfield and Preston waded noisily across, trailing three stout ropes behind them. They paused under the window, in the black shadow of the building, and listened. Wading the river in the pale shimmer of the starlight had been a ticklish business, and each heaved a sigh of relief when the profound gloom of the shadow swallowed them up.

As they strained their ears, a sound made itself evident, a rhythmic rumble that rose and fell without cessation. Suddenly it was punctuated by an explosive snort, then once again it resumed the unbroken tenor of its way.

"Hell," breathed Hatfield with a barely audible chuckle, "it's just the jailer snoring. Let him snore. He couldn't do anything to suit me better right now. All right, Preston, up you go."

He seized Preston about the thighs and without the least apparent effort hoisted him until his wet boots rested on the Ranger's sinewy shoulders.

"Garret's waitin' at the winder," Preston breathed down to him, "t'other feller's asleep. All right, pass me up the ropes."

Hatfield handed the wet lines to him, one by one, and Preston tied them securely to the stout window bars, which were set deeply in a heavy wooden frame. When the last was knotted tightly, the Ranger eased the ranch owner back into the water. Silently as before, they crept back across the river, their flesh crawling as the starlight revealed them plainly to any chance watcher, momentarily expecting a yell of alarm and the *whang* of a rifle. None came, however, nor did the hot pain of a bullet tearing through flesh and bone. Little Crowley swore his relief as they climbed, dripping, up the bank.

"All right," Hatfield told him as they mounted. "All together, now, not too fast . . . don't want to make a bronc' change ends. A good jerk at first, then a steady pull till the bars tear loose. That wood isn't never gonna hold against three good cutting hosses. Let's go!"

The ropes tightened with a hum like giant harp strings as the three big horses straightened them out and dug in their hoofs. Across the river sounded a *snapping* and *creaking*.

"She's comin'!" panted Hatfield. "Go to it, Goldy hoss! Give 'em hell, fellow!"

The giant sorrel snorted like a steam engine and gave a mighty lunge. From the direction of the jail sounded a rending *crash*. It was followed by a gigantic splintering and crackling, a tremendous splash, and a piercing yell muffled by thick wooden walls.

The splash subsided to a series of gurgling ripples, but the yells continued, gaining volume with every volley. There was also the sound of thrashing, thudding, wallowing, and gasping curses in Spanish and good United States.

"Good gosh-all-hemlock!" bawled Crowley. "The pull was too damn' much for that underpinnin' in back of the calaboose. It busted loose and dumped the whole thing inter the crick. Listen to that Mex jailer yell! His room is in the water and the door's on the side what's ag'in' the bottom. Good thing for him the water ain't deep!"

"Good thing for us the door is on the bottom!" growled Preston. "What's all that hell-a-fallutin' goin' on inside the calaboose? Sounds like a passel of wildcats havin' a free-for-all."

"It's one Texan and one Mexican havin' a free-for-all," Hatfield told him. "Tom Garret and that Mexican gambler's having a little party all their own. Wonder which head's coming out the window first?"

"I know which one better come out fust," replied Preston grimly, slipping his rifle from the boot.

"Somethin' better happen damn' quick!" bawled Crowley, climbing into his saddle with apprehension. "The hull town's woke up. Listen to 'em yell."

From inside the capsized jail sounded a hollow and watery *boom*.

"Damn' jailer's got a shotgun goin'!" grated Preston.

"What the hell's he shootin' at, fish?" demanded Crowley.

"You'll damn' soon find out, if he manages to get that door open," Hatfield replied. "Hell, those fellows on the

171

bank over there aren't shooting at fish! Let 'em have it. They spotted us!"

Bright flashes were rippling along the far bank of the creek. Rifles and six-guns crackled. Bullets whined about the trio on horseback. Almost before the first slug had screeched past, they were on the ground, their rifles blazing defiance to Cheno's followers.

Yells and shrieks went up as bullets found their mark. There was a rush of dark figures up the bank for cover. The Ranger strained his ears for the sound he most feared—the *click* of galloping hoofs.

"Somebody's comin' outta the jail!" bawled Preston, flinging up his rifle. He held a steady bead on the shadowy figure emerging from the splintered window, his eyes glowing hotly back of the sights. "Hell and dammit!" he exploded. "The damned sidewinder's done for Garret! Garret ain't got no whiskers!" Eyes insane with rage, his finger squeezed the trigger.

Crowley let out an agonized yell of warning.

XIII

"BORDER WAR"

Barely in time, Jim Hatfield knocked the rifle up. The bullet *whined* toward the stars, and Preston cursed like a madman. The Ranger's hair-trigger mind had interpreted the significance of Crowley's yell. He wrested the rifle from the ranch owner before he could direct a second shot at the form squirming madly through the narrow opening. "Garret's grown whiskers since he was locked up!" he roared in explanation.

"I'd forgot to tell you about it," chattered Crowley, between flinging shots across the creek. "Gawd, that was close!"

Preston's face was ghastly in the starlight. Hatfield shoved his own loaded rifle into his hands and began shoving cartridges into Preston's Winchester.

Garret was in the water now and foaming through it toward the bank. Bullets kicked up splashes and geysers all around him, but the withering fire of the three deadly rifles gave the Mexicans too much to think about to permit careful aim.

In a few seconds, Garret came clawing up the bank, water dripping from his scraggly gray beard and his long hair. Hatfield yelled directions as he flung Garret onto the spare horse, whose saddle consisted of a blanket roped to his bony back, and leaped on Goldy. The others also mounted in hot haste, still firing. Above the uproar could be heard the jailer's frenzied bawls and the reports of his shotgun as he tried to blast a way out of his watery prison.

But the Ranger had also heard another sound—the sound he dreaded. Horses were racing toward the creekbank. Even as rescuers and rescued got under way, a troop of Cheno's irregular cavalry stormed into the water.

"Ride!" the Ranger barked. "Never mind any more shootin'!"

Ride they did, through the pale shimmer of the starlight, heading for that far distant river to the north that spelled safety. The false dawn fled across the sky, and the black hour that follows it closed down. Still they pounded on, and still their pursuers held grimly on their trail. The borrowed horse that Tom Garret bestrode was beginning to falter.

Hatfield glanced anxiously behind. He could see the pursuit, irregular, dark blotches on the faintly glowing prairie.

To his left, looming gigantically against the darkling sky, was a range of wild hills. He had noticed those hills on the way into Mexico and knew they were gashed by cañons and gorges. With a word to the others, he slanted his speeding horse to the left.

"If we get in them hills, we'll get lost shore as hell," protested Crowley.

"And if we don't, we're gonna find ourselves in hell in less'n a hour," the Ranger told him. "It's our only chance to shake 'em off. They'll lose sight of us in those cañons, and they'll be scared to come riding hell-bent-for-leather after us and risk dry-gulchin'."

Perhaps Hatfield realized what the others did not—that it was the slower speed of their horses, particularly the one Garret bestrode, that was allowing the pursuers to continue their slow gain. But the Ranger gave that no consideration. His speed depended on the speed of the slowest horse of the four, for so long as one of his companions remained on the wrong side of the Río Grande, there, too, would be the Lone Wolf, battling alongside.

Swift minutes passed, and the black mouth of a cañon swallowed them up. On they sped at breakneck speed, risking a fall that would be fatal at every stride the gasping horses took. The cañon wound through the hills like a snake through a cactus patch. The mouth of a side cañon yawned, a darker patch in the shadowy wall. Hatfield unhesitatingly turned into it. A little farther on he led the way into still another narrow gorge.

The rosy glow of the true dawn was stealing across the sky when at last he called a halt on the banks of a brawling little stream that foamed from a narrow cleft in the gorge wall and plunged into another on the far side. While the horses drank and caught their wind, he slipped back down the cañon and listened. There was no sign of the pursuit.

"Calculate we've lost 'em," he muttered thankfully. "Likewise, I figure we've lost ourselves plumb proper."

They crossed the stream and rode on up the cañon for another hour. They had food enough in their saddlebags for a couple of meals, and, where an abrupt narrowing of the cañon walls made surprise by the pursuers almost impossible, they cooked and ate. Over the crude breakfast, the Ranger talked with Garret.

The rancher was not so old as he had at first surmised. His scraggly beard was streaked with gray, but there was none showing in his tawny hair. The resemblance between himself and his daughter was striking. Hatfield liked his brief word of thanks to all concerned in his rescue and his dismissal of the subject from then on.

"That damn' jigger in the jail with me tried to keep me from gettin' out," he explained about the row that was kicked up after the building tumbled into the water. "I got a notion he was planted there by Cheno to keep a eye on me. They was several of 'em in there durin' the past six months, all of 'em on some funny-soundin' charge. Soon as one would go out, 'nother would come in.

"There was other fellers there, too, ev'ry now and then, but they didn't stay long. Purty soon they was took out, and I'd hear rifles goin' off. They'd never come back. Calculate they was stood up 'gainst a wall and blowed loose from themselves. That was Cheno's way of gettin' rid of fellers that was in his way."

He paused, puffing hungrily on the cigarette Hatfield had rolled for him.

"I heerd some funny things from them fellers while I was in there," he added. "There's a merry hell gettin' ready to bust loose in these parts, or I'm much mistook. There's a real uprisin' 'gainst El Presidente in the makin' . . . one that's bein' managed proper and with a big man back of it.

"Money for it's been pourin' down from our side the Río Grande. Jest where it's comin' from I couldn't find out, but there's plenty of it. Cheno's got a real army gettin' t'gether, too. Them *soldados* in Tijerna ain't a piddlin' to what he's got back in the hills.

"I heard there was another army bein' got t'gether and drilled some place else. I don't know where, but it's a good one and armed with new rifles."

"I didn't calculate Cheno had the brains or get-up to pull any deal like that," pondered Preston.

Garret grunted scornfully. "He ain't," declared the owner of the Bowtie Ranch. "The feller back of all this is some really big and brainy jigger. Don't seem anybody knows his name. They call him The Rider."

Jim Hatfield, who had been listening intently to Garret's story, suddenly tensed, eyes narrowing, muscles rippling along his lean bronzed jaw. His mouth tightened like a bear trap, and his strangely colored eyes were cold as the sky of a rainy dawn as Garret repeated his last remark.

"Yeah, funny thing to call him, ain't it? But that's what they call him, jest El Caballero . . . The Rider."

XIV

"OUTLAW GUNS"

As they rode on through the morning sunlight, Jim Hatfield was silent and thoughtful. Many things that had puzzled him were beginning to become clear now, but it still remained a mystery who was the man behind the outrages

176

that had terrorized the bloody triangle. The Ranger had certain well-founded suspicions, but no proof that would stand up under the test. Pierce Kimble's face so like a death mask swam like an evil vision before his eyes, but so far there was nothing to connect the F Bar C foreman with any unlawful act.

That jigger may *have more brains than he looks to have,* he mused thoughtfully. *Well, I shore haven't got much to go on . . . a busted rifle cartridge and a little dust, but a fellow can trip over a busted shell and enough dust can be the makings of a grave. We'll let all that pass for a spell. Right now the big thing is to get out of this section of hell the devil forgot to shovel down below. It isn't going to be easy.*

It wasn't. Full three days passed before, half-starved and haggard with fatigue and lack of sleep, they sloshed through the shallow waters of the Río Grande and thankfully landed on Texas soil. Garret rode to the Circle P with them for clean clothes and a shave.

They found Tart Kearns in the ranch house with Hang Soon. Tart's usually good-natured face was set in hard lines.

"By Gawd, it's time you got back," was his greeting. "H'lo, Garret, where in hell did *you* come from? How'd you get outta the calaboose?"

"What's the matter, Tart?" asked Brant Preston. "Where's Hilton?"

"Dead," returned Kearns.

"Dead! Why, what the hell? What happened? How . . . ?"

"Pierce Kimble shot him," replied Kearns.

"What?"

"Uhn-huh, drilled him dead center."

Preston opened his mouth to shoot a barrage of questions. Jim Hatfield's cool tones stopped him.

"Suppose," suggested the Ranger, "we let Tart start at the beginning and tell us what happened."

Preston nodded silently, a little surprised at Hatfield's taking the lead.

" 'Twas like this," began Kearns. "We was in Flintlock Finnegan's place havin' a drink or two. Pierce Kimble come in. Him and Hank got to chawin' the rag, and Pierce said somethin' nasty to Hank. Jest what it was I don't know, but it was so damn' bad that Hank went right straight for his gun."

"And Pierce beat him to the draw?" interpolated Wes Crowley.

"Beat him to the draw? Hell, Pierce didn't even move till Hank's hawgleg cleared leather. Then he pulled and shot Hank 'fore Hank could pull trigger. He was so damn' fast you couldn't see his hand move hardly. It was jest plain murder. Poor ol' Hank didn't never have a chanct, and Pierce knowed he wouldn't have none.

"Pierce let Hank get his gun out first so's nobody couldn't make nothin' of it but self-defense . . . but jest the same it was plain murder. I was so damn' mad I started to go for him myself, but Spud Bacon and Chuck Holly from the Bowtie was there, and they grabbed me. I fought like hell to get loose, and Kimble jest stood, waitin'. When he saw I couldn't make it, he looked sorta disappointed and walked out.

"I reckon Spud and Chuck saved my bacon for me. Pierce would've killed me jest as easy as he did poor Hank. Goddermighty, but he's fast! And he used the funniest draw I ever seed . . . a cross-draw from a side holster! I allus thought them guns of his'n hung funny, but I never knowed why till I saw him go for one."

Jim Hatfield suddenly stared at the speaker, a queer light in his eyes.

"Did you say he pulls across?" the Ranger asked, his voice tense and sharp.

"Uhn-huh, pulls acrost like you would if the hawgleg was stuck in your belt."

Brant Preston was blazing with rage: "By Gawd, I'll see about this! I'm gonna hunt that corpse-faced sidewinder up and blow him out from under his hat! He can't kill my men like that and get away with it!"

Hatfield's quiet voice bit at him. "No, you're not, Preston. You wouldn't have a chance."

"Like hell I wouldn't!" barked the ranch owner. "I'm one hell of a sight faster than Hank Hilton ever thought of bein'. He won't wait for me to clear leather 'fore he pulls."

"Yeah, I know you aren't slow," Jim Hatfield replied with authority. "I saw you pull that night in the *cantina,* and you aren't bad, but just the same I'm sayin' you wouldn't have a chance. Preston, did you ever hear of Bill Graham?"

"Hell, who ain't?" replied Preston. "He was the wuss killer and fastest man on the draw in Arizona. Hung out over Tombstone way."

"Yeah, that's right. Do you happen to recollect that Bill Graham used a cross-draw from a side holster, one of the few men who ever did?"

"Shore, I heerd he did. But what's that got to do with Pierce Kimble? The Earps and Doc Holliday killed Bill Graham alongside a water hole in Arizona."

"The Earps claimed they did," corrected Hatfield. "Nobody ever found Graham's body. Wyatt Earp himself only said that he cut loose on Bill Graham with a double charge of buckshot, and Bill yelled and dropped back of a rock. Lots of folks claim he snuck out of Arizona because things were getting too hot . . . that he wasn't killed a-tall, mebbe not even wounded."

"But hell, feller," protested Preston, "Bill Graham was a big beefy jigger with black whiskers. Pierce Kimble ain't got no whiskers, and he's thin as a roadrunner."

"Whiskers come off pretty easy with a razor, and it isn't hard to keep 'em off. Fellows sometimes lose their fat when they get older, especially if they happen to be shot up bad like mebbe Bill Graham was. And listen . . . I've seen Bill Graham once, listened to him talk. He had that same funny slow way of smilin' Pierce Kimble's got, only with whiskers you didn't notice it so much.

"Sort of funny, don't you think, that a jigger should have that same sort of unusual way of grinnin' and use the same kind of draw, which mighty few men ever use and hardly no one ever gets to working it real fast. Don't you think it's funny, Preston?"

For a minute Brant Preston hesitated, then he swore helplessly. "I've got half a notion you're right, and, if you are, I'll bet my last steer that hellion is out to finish off the whole Circle P outfit. He knows, if he can force a fight with us one at a time, he can do it easy. What the hell we gonna do 'bout it?"

"We'll talk about that a little later," Hatfield replied. "Now, Brant, I want you to promise me something . . . a little favor for me."

Brant Preston looked oddly at the man who stood before him. There was something that commanded attention in him.

"Hell," growled Preston, "after what you did for us t'other side the river, I ain't refusin' you nothin'. What you want?"

"I want you to promise me you won't go looking for Kimble till I say it is all right, and that goes for you, Wes, and you, Tart."

"I promise," returned Preston gloomily, "and the boys will, too. But I don't see what in hell we're gonna do."

Tom Garret rode on to the Bowtie and a joyful reunion with his daughter. Hatfield and the Circle P boys went to bed. The Ranger first scrubbed the stain from his face and hands. Water would not affect it, but plenty of strong soap did.

The others were still asleep when the Ranger ate a hurried breakfast that Hang Soon threw together for him, saddled Goldy, and headed for Cuevas. All day he loafed about the town, chiefly in Flintlock Finnegan's saloon, apparently waiting for somebody. Men came and went. Sheriff Raines came in, scowled blackly at him, had a drink, and went out again.

Hatfield stifled a grin at the old fire-eater's by-play and returned Hipless Harley's half-humorous nod. Still he lingered at the bar, watching the swinging doors.

It was nearly dark, and the hanging lamps were casting their beams over the gathering crowd when he suddenly stepped away from the bar and walked to the middle of the big room. Pierce Kimble had just slithered through the swinging doors. He paused for an instant, and his eyes singled out the Ranger's tall form.

The occupants of the room sensed something unusual. Their chatter died to a low hum, then ceased altogether. In the silence that followed, the Lone Wolf's voice rang clear, barbed with insult.

"Hello, murderer," he called. "Looking for another slow old man to kill?"

Pierce Kimble's long body stiffened. He stared at Hatfield, his face livid, his black eyes crawling with reddish fire. The Ranger's voice bit at him again.

"Reckon Tombstone got to have a sort of final sound for you, didn't it? So you came east a spell to find . . . a grave, eh, *Bill Graham?*"

For a paralyzed instant, men stood gasping at the sound of the noted outlaw's name. Then there was a wild scramble to get out of line. Down and across flashed Pierce Kimble's hand, in the draw that no living man had ever beaten and few equaled.

Jim Hatfield, lightning fast though he knew himself to be, did not try to beat it. His slim hands did not even move in the direction of his Colts. Like a released spring, he went across the room directly toward Kimble's flaming gun, dodging, slewing, weaving, like a shadow glancing across a ripple.

Blood spurted from his cheek where one of Kimble's bullets grazed the flesh. His hat was swept from his head; one sleeve was ripped to shreds. Then with a hurricane blast of sound, both his heavy sixes let go.

The stream of lead literally lifted Kimble from his feet and blasted him into eternity with his finger still twitching on the trigger of his empty gun. He crashed to the floor almost at the Lone Wolf's feet, one spearhead hand reaching toward the Ranger's boot.

The saloon was a pandemonium. Men were yelling, shouting, laughing hysterically.

"Didja ever see anythin' like it?"

"He walked right smack inter them bullets and dodged 'em comin'!"

"Hell, he was jest givin' Kimble a chanct. He could've throwed his guns up in the air, caught 'em comin' down, and plugged Pierce 'fore he could clear leather!"

"Gents, that was shootin'!"

Hatfield knelt beside the dead man and turned him over

on his back. Silently he opened the other's shirt and stared at the mass of puckered scars marking his breast.

"Feller," Flintlock Finnegan asked, "was he really Bill Graham?"

"I don't know for shore," Hatfield admitted, "but he had eyes and hands and a grin like Graham's, and he drew crossways like Graham. And you'll recollect, Wyatt Earp always claimed he shot Graham in the breast with a double charge of buckshot, and, well, those scars alongside his wishbone shore look to me like they were made by buckshot."

"They shore do," agreed the old saloonkeeper. "What I'd like to know," he muttered to himself as he stood up, "is who the hell, big feller, are *you?*"

XV

"BLOODY GOLD"

Hatfield walked to the sheriff's office and surrendered. Flintlock Finnegan went with him and testified that the shots had been fired in self-defense. The Ranger remained with the sheriff for further questioning after Flintlock left.

"Now what the hell's it all about?" asked Sheriff Raines when the door had closed on the saloonkeeper. Hatfield told him.

"Yeah, the Hilton killin' was bad," agreed the sheriff, "but there wasn't anythin' I could do about it. Everybody swore it was self-defense. I heerd *Don* Fernando was terrible put out about it. They say he lit on Kimble with all four feet. Folks said they thought Kimble would draw on him for what he said, but they finally patched it up.

"Cartina sets a heap of store by Kimble . . . I heerd Kimble saved his life onct somehow or other, never did learn jest how. The *don* ain't the kind of a feller what forgets a thing like that."

Hatfield nodded absently, his thoughts evidently elsewhere.

"Sheriff, how big a posse can you get together in a hurry, if I happen to need them bad?" he asked suddenly.

Sheriff Raines ruminated. "Calculate I can count on about thirty gents, more or less," he decided. "That be enough?"

"It'll have to be," replied the Ranger. "No, I don't know when I'll need 'em . . . not yet. May not need 'em a-tall, but, if I do, I'll need 'em bad."

"By the way," remarked the sheriff, "I got some letters here for you . . . been sev'ral days."

Hatfield read the letters. When he had finished, he sat for some time staring into nothing. Finally he turned to the sheriff.

"Calculate I'm liable to need that posse pretty soon, after all," he said. "Well, how're chances to sleep in your jail tonight? I'm pretty well tuckered and want a good bed."

Jim Hatfield did sleep in the jail, with plenty of blankets and a good mattress. The next morning he rode to *Don* Fernando Cartina's F Bar C ranch.

"I calculated I'd better ride out and have a little talk with you about what happened last night," he explained to the ranch owner, who met him at the verandah steps and invited him into the ranch house with grave courtesy.

"I'm sorry it happened," said Cartina frankly. "I felt a heavy debt of gratitude to Kimble, but I am forced to admit there were times when he sorely tried my patience. The revelation that he was undoubtedly the notorious outlaw,

Graham, was the last straw. I feel that you were justified in what you did."

"I'm shore glad to hear that," Hatfield replied. "I was hoping you wouldn't hold it against me."

"Certainly not," *Don* Fernando assured him heartily but sadly. "Wait, you must have something to eat and drink before you ride back to town. Just a minute, and I'll make arrangements."

He hurried toward the back of the house, and Hatfield was left alone in the big, comfortably furnished room. Swiftly his eyes ran over it, noting everything of interest. His gaze traveled keenly over a rifle lying in antler prongs above the fireplace.

When *Don* Fernando reëntered the room, Hatfield from the corner of his eye noted the haggard, worried look on the ranch owner's face. He turned suddenly, looking the other straight in the eye.

"Cartina," he said softly, "I'm plumb sorry I had to kill your half-brother."

Don Fernando gasped. "So . . . so you know!" The Mexican's voice was heavy with dread.

"Yes," Hatfield replied. "I learned your mother's name was Graham before she married your father. It wasn't hard to tie things up after that."

"We were boys together," *Don* Fernando said dully. "My mother loved him. He was the elder, but I was always steadier. She . . . she left him in my care when she died, or thought she did. You know what happened. He came here after the Earps and Holliday nearly killed him. Most people believed he was dead. I guess it would have been better if he had died when Earp shot him."

The Ranger's face was grim when he replied. "Yes, it would have."

★ ★ ★ ★ ★

A little later he rode back to Cuevas, his black brows furrowed. There was a single gunsmith in Cuevas, a taciturn old fellow with a genius for minding his own business. The Ranger felt he could be trusted to keep his mouth shut. He showed the old man his star and asked some questions.

The gunsmith wrinkled his brow, thought for a moment, and answered the questions with precision. Then he rummaged in a box of junk and finally drew forth a bit of steel. The Ranger took it, glanced at it, and uttered an exclamation of satisfaction. He shook hands with the gunsmith, and left the dusty shop. Later he had a talk with Darnel, the cashier of the Cuevas bank. Dark found him at the Circle P ranch house.

The news of the killing had preceded him, and Brant Preston and the boys were loud in their congratulations and praise. Tom Garret was there, and Lonnie. The girl shyly thanked him for the rescue of her father. Hatfield grinned down at her and changed the subject. His eyes were brooding, however, when she and Brant Preston rode away together. Back of those gray-green eyes dread plans were afoot.

Day after day Hatfield rode the Circle P range. Also, unknown to the Circle P waddies and Preston, he rode through the many little river villages that hugged the banks of the Río Grande. In the role of a wandering cowboy, he drank in the *cantinas*, danced with dark-eyed *señoritas*, and wagered on cockfights.

Everywhere he was greeted with true Mexican courtesy and hospitality. The Lone Wolf had a way with him, and the naïve villagers confided many secrets, but the thing he sought eluded him. There was one subject the villagers would not discuss. Veiled allusions produced only tight-lipped silence.

Over the apparently light-hearted little pueblos brooded something ominous and terrible. The Lone Wolf could sense a tense expectancy, a waiting for something dreaded and feared about to happen. It was as the lull that precedes the storm. Plainly the villagers were afraid—afraid, and fascinated by portending events. Hatfield was worried, and the dull gray deepened in his eyes.

I calculate I can chop the head off the damned snake almost any time, he told himself, *but, even if I do, the tail's liable to wiggle till the sun goes down and cause plenty of trouble. I've just naturally got to drop my loop on the whole critter at once. But how the hell am I going to do that when I don't even know for sure what I'm twirling my rope at?*

Finally he gave up on the villages and turned his attention to the Cingaro Trail. Through grim, bone-strewn Pardusco Cañon he followed the crooked track, losing himself amid the maze of branches that tortured through narrow gorges and side cañons, the thing he sought always eluding him.

One night, as he sat Goldy in the shadow of a mesquite thicket, a large band of riders thundered past, the irons of their horses striking sparks from the stones. He tried to follow the band, but a heavy rain was falling, washing out what few tracks they made, and the roar of white water in the cañon drowned the sounds of hoofs. Somewhere amid the tangle of trails he lost them.

In the meanwhile, things happened. A bullion shipment left Cuevas secretly and in the dead of night, the gold masquerading as beans, flour, and other supplies in a small rancher's wagon. At daybreak, a score of miles along the north trail, it was raided and the gold carried off. The rancher and his companion, shot from ambush, didn't even have a chance to draw their guns. It was a heavy loss to the two Cuevas mines whose shipment it was.

"It seems there is no such thing as secrecy or safety any more," *Don* Fernando Cartina told Sheriff Raines while discussing the robbery. "Very few persons, apparently, knew anything about that shipment. The men who were supposed to know are above suspicion, but evidently someone else knew or guessed. Have you any clues, Sheriff?"

Sheriff Raines was forced to admit he hadn't.

Jim Hatfield rode to the spot where the robbery had occurred and, after a painstaking search, unearthed two recently exploded cartridge cases. He examined them with care and compared them with the one he had found when Curly Wilkes was dry-gulched, noting a difference that narrowed his green eyes.

I wonder if I've got any business leaving that damned sidewinder loose and fanging? he pondered. *If I'd grabbed him before now, maybe those two poor devils would be alive. Hell, it's damned hard to know just what to do sometimes.*

In a snug hide-out along the Pardusco Trail, a bloated spider of a man with beady black eyes and a merciless mouth pawed gold ingots with greedy hands and chuckled softly to himself.

"*Maldito,* this is the great help," he addressed his companion, who sat on the far side of the table, sombrero pulled low over his glinting eyes, serape muffled about his chin. "Soon, *amigo mío,* we will be able to strike. And then. . . ."

He licked his thick lips with anticipation and caressed the dull-colored bars. The other nodded, but said nothing.

XVI

"PIT OF HELL"

The Ranger continued to ride the Cingaro Trail, prowling the side cañons, striking into the hills at times—searching, searching! He came upon a few lonely, deserted cabins, where prospectors had burrowed industriously into the hillsides or on the banks of little streams.

Sometimes there was evidence that the gold seekers had acquired modest wealth. More often the story was one of disappointment or tragedy, with rusting tools amid the grass or a caved-in shaft or tunnel. Once or twice he found moldering bones.

Then one day he approached a little clearing at no great distance from the main trail. He halted for a moment as a thin wail shattered the silence.

Again the sound came, faint, hollow. It was a voice, a human voice fraught with terror and despair. Over and over the single word sounded: "*¡Ayuda! ¡Ayuda!* Help! Help!"

Hatfield spurred forward swiftly, shouting as he rode. He tried to locate the sound, but it was elusive, apparently coming from the ground beneath his horse's hoofs. Abruptly he pulled Goldy to a halt once more and swung from the saddle. He had caught sight of the earth-ringed, yawning mouth of an ancient mine shaft.

"Looks like some poor devil's fallen down that hole," he muttered, hastening toward the opening. "Hold on, pardner!" he shouted. "I'm comin' *pronto!*"

He reached the shaft and peered into it. For a tense moment he hung over the dank hole, his flesh crawling, a sickly feeling at the pit of his stomach. Unconsciously he drew back, a slight shiver twitching his big shoulders.

"God, is there anything they won't do?" he breathed. He leaned over the shaft lip again, his face grim. "Don't move, feller," he called. "Take it easy right where you are. I'll get you out some way! For God's sake *don't move!*"

The shaft was not deep, scarcely more than eight feet, with a smooth, damp floor. It was some six feet in diameter. At the bottom stood a man who pressed his scrawny body against the crumbling dirt wall. He stood utterly motionless on bare feet, his ragged pantaloons rolled above his knees, his arms bound tightly to his side by turn on turn of rawhide. He was evidently on the verge of collapse from exhaustion and fear. He stood utterly motionless in his strained position, and for good cause.

On the floor of the shaft, restlessly moving, gliding here and gliding there, vainly seeking escape from their prison, there were fully a dozen huge mountain rattlesnakes. From time to time one slithered over the miserable captive's bare feet or brushed against the shrinking flesh of his leg.

"Don't move," Hatfield cautioned him again, knowing that as long as he stood like a statue he was fairly safe from the reptiles. But let him shift a foot or reel from exhaustion, and the needle-sharp fangs, dripping venom like brown ink, would be plunged into his flesh.

For a moment the Ranger stood racking his brain. He half drew one of his guns, and let it fall back in its holster. He might shoot all the snakes, despite the difficult angle and the uncertain light, but the risk of wounding instead of killing outright was too great. The rattlers, lashing about in pain and terror, were almost certain to strike the hapless *peón.* No he couldn't take such chances. There was but one thing to do.

Searching about, he found a stout club. He hefted it for weight, ran his eye along it in quest of a flaw in the wood, and found none. Next he called Goldy, unlooped his reata, and made sure it was tied hard and fast. For an instant he was tempted to try and drop the loop over the *peón's* shoulders and jerk him out of the pit before the snakes could strike, but again he decided the risk was too great. Had the man's arms not been bound, it would have been comparatively simple, but as it was, there was always the chance that the noose might slip and the helpless victim fall back on top of the snakes. No, there was but one thing to do.

"Steady, hoss," he cautioned. Wrapping the rope about one arm and holding the club, he raised his hands high above his head and leaped down into that pit of horror.

He landed squarely on a big rattler, smashing the life out of it instantly. Another threw itself into a loose fold and struck with lightning speed. The fangs clashed harmlessly against the tough leather of the Ranger's high boots. The club swept down and beat the snake to death before it could strike again.

Back against the helpless *peón,* shielding him from a chance strike, the Lone Wolf fought a nightmare battle in that pit of hell. All about him buzzed and hissed the madly aroused reptiles. Time and again they struck, and time and time again his tough boots saved him. He was pretty sure that none of the rattlers could strike high enough to get above the protecting leather, but he was not absolutely sure, and the possibility made his flesh crawl.

One huge reptile, rearing high, lashed at the club as it descended. His long fangs stabbed the tough wood a scant inch from the Ranger's hand—so close, in fact, that the released venom splashed his fingers.

Hatfield was soon dripping with sweat, and he thought

he would suffocate in the close air of the pit, reeking as it was with the horrible stench of the milling reptiles. Again and again he struck, his arm aching and burning with fatigue, his nerves taut to the breaking point. It seemed to him that the devilish things multiplied with each blow.

Hatfield had already killed so many, and still, it seemed, there were as many as at the beginning. In a red haze he slashed and pounded and stamped in that nightmare inferno of writhing bodies and gaping jaws.

Abruptly he realized that he was pounding a dead snake to pulp. There were no more live reptiles left to face him. Gasping for breath, he turned to the captive. The *peón* suddenly gave a choking cry and groveled against the wall. Hatfield followed his bulging eyes and saw a last rattler, dying with a broken back, lying across the man's foot.

The Ranger saw also the ominous twin punctures that marked where the fangs had pierced the naked ankle in a last convulsive movement. Cursing bitterly, he ground the snake's head to fragments with his boot heel. Then he draped the *peón*'s sagging body across his shoulder and went up the rope, hand over hand, Goldy snorting and bearing back against the lunging weight.

Reaching the surface, Hatfield slashed the rawhide thongs that bound the *peón*'s arms, laid him on the ground, and went to work on the wound. He applied a tourniquet made with a handkerchief, slashed the fang punctures crisscross, laid his lips to the wound, and sucked out as much blood as possible. A little stream ran through the clearing, and in this he dipped his neckerchief and applied it to the wound as a wet dressing to stimulate draining.

The *peón* was dazed to near unconsciousness by pain, terror, and exhaustion. He was a scrawny little fellow with soft brown eyes and the mouth of an abused child. The

Lone Wolf stared down at him compassionately. He knew the kind—there were many, many like him in the river villages—children, despite the years of manhood, who needed care and gentle supervision, yet in them the making of good citizens. Looking after such people and seeing to it that they received justice was part of a Ranger's work. Easily influenced, they were a potential asset or liability to the state, according to whose hand shaped them.

"And of late there's been too many devil claws tendin' to the job," the Ranger growled, his face bleak.

Almost hidden in a tangle of burr oaks was the deserted mine cabin, old, dilapidated, but still secure against wind and weather. Hatfield found it to be furnished with a rusty little stove, a rickety table and chairs, and a bunk built against the wall. He cut boughs, filled the bunk with them, and laid his saddle blanket over them, making a fairly comfortable bed for the patient.

Soon he had a fire going in the stove and heated water in a battered tin bucket he unearthed. He had a little food in his saddlebags, including coffee, and a small skillet and coffee pot.

There was a chance, he knew, that the fiends who had placed the *peón* in the snake pit might come back to see how their victim was faring, but he decided not to risk it even though he rather relished the idea of a brush with them. He loosely tethered Goldy, deep in the pine grove, where he could graze and roll and still be safe from possible theft. Then he went back to spend the night attending the wants of his patient. Wise in the ways of the forest, he brewed a draft from roots, leaves, and berries he had gathered and forced the injured man to swallow it.

The drink had an almost immediate effect. A little color crept back into the sallow face; the lips lost their ghastly gray tinge. The man opened his eyes and stared at Jim, uncomprehendingly at first. Then remembrance flooded his brain, and he struggled to sit up.

"Take it easy," Jim Hatfield soothed him. "You're all right now. Nothing to worry about. Just take it easy."

Still the *peón* struggled to speak. Finally the words came, sliding over his stiff lips in a froth of terror.

"Rosa!" he gasped, ". . . *mujer* . . . Rosa!"

Hatfield leaned closer. "What about your wife Rosa?" he asked.

The black eyes were like those of a hunted animal. "*¡Los caballeros!* They ride to Canales! They kill her!"

For a moment the Ranger sat silently, thinking furiously. Canales was a river village, many hours of hard riding distant. It would take him all night to reach the little pueblo and rescue the woman from the vengeance of the riders. He very much feared that, if left alone during the night, the *peón* would die. There was also the deadly danger that the devils who had placed him in the snake pit might return, seek him out, and finish him. His life was too valuable to risk. The Lone Wolf was confident that in this little, timid bit of humanity he had the key to El Hombre's hidden stronghold. No, there was too much at stake. He could not leave the *peón* for the night—there had to be another way.

Suddenly he exclaimed sharply under his breath. "Why didn't I think of it before!" he exulted. "Tom Garret'll be glad to hustle down to Canales and do this little chore for me. He can grab off the girl and take her back to the Bowtie with him. She'll be safe there . . . nobody'll know about what happened here." He asked: "Your name, *amigo?* Where does your wife live in Canales?"

"The house on the little hill by the river . . . the first house when one rides from the west," whispered the other.

"You will save her, *señor?* Me, I am Doreto."

"Yes, I'll see she's taken care of," Hatfield promised simply. "Now you just take another swallow of this stuff and go to sleep. I'll be back in a little while. Just take it easy."

The Bowtie ranch house was less than an hour of fast riding from the cañon. Hatfield made Goldy sift sand, and there was still a glow of the sunset above the western peaks when he pulled up at the Bowtie, swung to the ground, and hurried up the verandah. Light steps sounded in answer to his knock, and Lonnie Garret opened the door. She gave a little cry of pleasure at sight of her visitor.

"Your dad?" Hatfield asked after greeting her. "I want to see him, right away."

"He is in Cuevas," Lonnie replied. "He and the boys rode in this afternoon. They won't be back until late. I'm all by myself except for Teresa, the cook."

XVII

"THROUGH THE DARK HOURS"

For a tense moment Hatfield stared at Lonnie Garret, his whole plan tumbling about his ears. The girl sensed something was wrong, and her face grew anxious.

"What is it?" she asked. "You're worried about something."

Hatfield hesitated before speaking. Then he decided to take a chance. In terse sentences he told her what had happened. He held out his Ranger's star to her astonished gaze.

For a moment she looked mutely at the silver star. A

Ranger! Lonnie Garret looked awestruck.

"So you see how mighty important it is for me to get back to that hollow and be with the poor fellow," he concluded, "and still I can't let him down about his wife. I promised him I'd look out for her. Now what the blazes am I going to do? You think you could get to Cuevas in time to round up your dad and send him to Canales?"

"No," replied the red-haired girl instantly and decisively. "I'm not even going to try. Wait here."

She was through the door and halfway down the verandah steps when Hatfield's shout reached her.

"What're you doing? Where're you going?"

"I'm going to Canales. Wait until I saddle my horse!"

She was at the corral, whistling a clear note, before the Ranger caught up with her.

"You can't do that, Lonnie," he protested as a clean-limbed little pinto came trotting to the bars, whinnying a question. "You can't take a chance. You're just as liable as not to run into those riders."

"I'm taking it," she replied briefly, flinging down the corral bars. "If you can take the chances you do for people who really mean practically nothing to you, I can take a little one for those who mean a great deal to me. After all, I live here and . . . and . . . others live here!"

Her cheeks were bright with color as she finished, but she smiled up at him as she led the pony to the stable and flung her saddle on his back.

The Ranger said briefly, his gray-green eyes warm with admiration: "All right, little lady, have your own way about it. Listen, you'll have to take a spare horse along for the girl to ride . . . can't take any chances on your pony carryin' double. You might have to make a run for it. No, wait, I got a better notion. Will your pony follow if you're on another hoss?"

"Yes," she replied. "He is trained to."

"All right," Hatfield told her, "that's fine." He whistled to Goldy, who came trotting to him. "Up you go!" he exclaimed, tossing her lightly onto the sorrel's back. "He'll take you there faster'n anything in Texas. Don't run your own horse to death. Hold Goldy in and give yours a chance. You've got time to make it, I'm shore. Those other hellions won't hustle . . . they'll figure they've got all the time in the world."

"Get my rifle from over the mantel," said Lonnie, as she pulled the weapon from the saddle scabbard. "Here, take yours, mine is lighter and I handle it better. There are spare saddles in the barn. That roan over there is a good pony . . . take him."

A moment later she was speeding swiftly down the white trail, the pinto, reins festooned from the bit, stirrups jingling, pounding along a few strides behind the great sorrel. The Lone Wolf watched her out of sight, then he roped the roan, saddled up, and headed back to the cañon cabin and his all-night vigil with his patient.

Through the lovely blue dusk, the shimmer of the stars, and then the silvery flood of the moonlight raced the girl, the miles unrolling their white ribbon behind her. Midnight came and went. The great clock in the sky wheeled on from east to west.

Clouds began unveiling the moon at times, and the prairie grew shadowy and mysterious. Finally the pale gleam of the river showed on her left. Another half hour and she slowed the sorrel. Directly ahead was the village of Canales.

On a little knoll loomed the hut of Doreto, the *peón*. It was silent and dark. Lonnie wondered if she were in time, or if the raiders had already done their work. The cold stillness of death seemed to brood over the little home, but when she knocked on the barred door, a frightened voice answered.

Quickly she explained to the Mexican woman. A moment later Doreto's wife slipped through the doorway. She was a shy little thing with great dark eyes that were now black pools of terror, but with Indian stoicism she accepted the danger that threatened her.

"*Sí*, I can ride," she answered Lonnie's question. "I am ready."

She mounted lithely and took the reins Lonnie handed her.

"Hush," she whispered, "someone comes!"

Lonnie heard it, too—the pound of swift hoofs ascending the knoll. Out of the shadows loomed ghostly riders, barring the way.

"*¡Alto!*" a voice shouted.

Instantly the red-haired girl went into action. "Follow me!" she called to the Mexican woman.

Dropping the reins on Goldy's neck, knowing that the intelligent horse would know what to do, she jerked her rifle from the boot and charged straight at the approaching group, the saddle gun streaming flame.

There was a yell of pain and fear, a confused trampling of hoofs as the horses shied away from the spurts of fire and the screeching bullets. Another man shrieked in agony and pitched from the saddle. His horse wheeled and fled madly, adding to the confusion.

Before the astounded killers could catch their breath, the two women were through their disordered ranks and scudding down the rise. Bullets *whined* after them, and a volley of curses, but to Goldy's iron endurance the long hours of travel had meant nothing, while the pinto, which had carried no load, was comparatively fresh.

Behind sounded the *click* of hoofs that soon died to a whisper of sound and ceased altogether. With the red dawn flaming behind them and the blue ripple of the wind tossing grasses in front, the two women rode to the distant Bowtie and safety.

I'll just wager he will be proud of me now! Lonnie thought to herself. Her cheeks were bright with color, and her eyes as dream-filled as the dawn.

At the cabin in the cañon, the Lone Wolf spent a busy night with his patient. Morning found the *peón* weak, in considerable pain, his leg much swollen, but alive. The Ranger's prompt and skillful doctoring had saved his life, and he would not lose his leg.

Leaving him to sleep fitfully, Hatfield scouted about the clearing and the grove and managed to knock over a brace of blue grouse with a Colt. He scoured the bucket thoroughly and made broth, which he fed to the patient. Then he risked a quick ride to the Bowtie ranch house.

Tom Garret was there, and the cowboys. Garret was well-nigh bursting with pride at his daughter's exploit. Once the 'punchers had departed for the bunkhouse, Hatfield took Garret into his confidence and secured his promise of secrecy.

"You're a real partner," he told Lonnie as he swung onto Goldy's back, "and you're going to make a real wife for one of the finest men I ever met."

The day passed uneventfully in the cañon, and the night. On the morning of the second day, the Ranger decided that the *peón* was strong enough to ride. Sitting beside him, he questioned him gently.

At first, terror filmed the dark eyes and the man would not talk. Gradually, however, under the hypnotic influence of the Lone Wolf's steady eyes and quiet voice, halting words came forth, became coherent, steadied to a story fantastic, weird, and amazing, a grim story of horror and cruelty, of towering, ruthless ambition and ingenious planning. No longer were the riders and El Hombre a mystery.

The whole sinister business was now an open page to the lean, stern-faced lieutenant of Rangers. Now, he, too, had the information he most needed. Already he was busy making a plan, a plan that would free the bloody triangle country from the dark blight that was settling over it and tear loose the cruel grip of the ill-omened night-flitting riders and El Hombre.

Hatfield took his patient in to Cuevas and turned him over to Jed Raines. The kindly old sheriff clucked sympathetically and proceeded to make the fellow comfortable.

"You're safe here," the Ranger assured Doreto. "So you just wanted to leave the outfit for a while so you could see your wife? And because of that they shoved you in that hole and threw the snakes in with you?

"Well, quite a few snakes passed out the other day, and they're quite a few more who are going to get something of the same dose, or I'm much mistaken. I'll see that Rosa remains safe. We'll bring her here if she isn't too worn out to come.

"Don't you worry, *amigo*, everything's going to be all right. Now let's go over those directions again of how to get to the hang-out of the sidewinders."

XVIII

"THE LONE WOLF RIDES"

The Ranger headed back to the Cingaro Trail. He paused first at the Circle P storehouse for some things he felt he needed. Preston had a good supply of dynamite on hand, to be used for blowing water holes. Hatfield stuffed his saddlebags with carefully wrapped sticks. He also took caps and a big coil of fuse.

He rode through Pardusco Cañon, carefully checking certain landmarks. Finally he turned into a narrow, sunless gorge, and continued warily. Finally, just as the sunset was flaring golden behind the western peaks, he passed from the narrow neck into a wide, almost circular bowl ringed about by low cliffs, the hills tumbling up beyond.

It was silent and deserted now, but the grass had been ground from the dusty earth by the endless passing and repassing of countless bare feet and the hoofs of many horses. The Lone Wolf could envision the brown ranks forming and reforming, going through endless military maneuvers under watchful eyes whose owners thought nothing of condemning a hapless bungler to the torturous death of cactus crucifixion or ant hill.

Watchful, alert, he crossed the open space to the low cliffs on the far side. Here, after a little searching, he found what he sought.

Skillfully concealed by bushes and vines was the dark opening of a cave. The sides and roof had been timbered. The floor was smooth and dry. The Ranger entered it, lighting a bit of candle he had brought with him. A dozen steps farther on he paused and stared at what the flickering flame revealed.

Rifles, hundreds of them, new, carefully greased, and stacked, and box after box of ammunition. From floor to timbered roof, the long rows stretched across the cave.

For minutes the Ranger gazed at the arms, visualizing what they meant. He saw the border seething with blood and flame—murder, lust, and robbery rampant, the killings, the torturings.

He saw, too, what would come later—the thundering horses of the blue-clad cavalrymen of the Union, surging through the river villages, their sabers flashing in the sun, their pistols flaming in the night. The peaceful little river villages, no longer peaceful, would be lashed to a mad fury by cruelty and terror and the ruthless ambition of a twisted mind.

The tall Ranger set about to thwart that ambition and prevent the horror that was in the making. Carefully, skillfully, he planted his dynamite, concealing it from possible prying eyes and just as skillfully concealing the snaky length of fuse that ran from the cave to the summit of the low, slanting cliff.

He calculated just how long it would take the fuse to burn and just how long it would take him to reach the narrow entrance of the clearing from the cliff top. The coil proved ample for the purpose.

Then, with the stage set for the drama that would be exacted the following night, he rode back to Cuevas.

There was excitement when he got there, after midnight.

"They hit the bank this time!" a bartender told him excitedly. "Cleaned it out proper. Old Ab Carlyle wasn't there with his scatter-gun this time, poor ol' devil. Darnel did what he could, but he was too slow. They bent a gun barrel over his haid, tied up the clerks, and took fifty thousand dollars. Jed Raines is chasin' 'em through the hills, but they got a good start, and I don't calculate Jed has much chance."

Jim Hatfield frowned at what he saw. It was a threat to the success of his plan. He was much relieved when Hipless Harley rode in a little later. Harley had been to Crater and did not know about the robbery.

"Now listen close," Hatfield told him, "here's what I want you to do. . . ."

He drew a map on the tablecloth and explained in detail the route to the cliff-walled amphitheater in the hills.

"It's up to you to round up Raines and the posse and bring 'em there," he concluded. "Mebbe you can run him down. Me, I'll stay in Cuevas till the last minute on the chance of his comin' back."

"And if he don't show up, you're ridin' inter that nest of sidewinders by yourself?" questioned Harley in an awed voice.

"Yeah," the Lone Wolf replied simply. "You see, I'm used to ridin' alone, and it's my job."

Hatfield found Darnel, the bank cashier and acting president, at his desk. Darnel had a split scalp and a nasty headache, but otherwise he was in pretty good shape.

"Yes, I got a reply to that letter you asked me to write to the Frisco bank," he answered Hatfield's question. "Here it is . . . they gave the name of the companies they've been making out drafts to, according to instructions. Does that help you any?"

The Ranger glanced at the names of noted arms dealers, and nodded.

"Uhn-huh, this is about the last knot in the hog-tying. It's just about all I needed to tighten my loop."

"This robbery will just about knock the props from under the bank, Hatfield," the cashier worried.

"Never mind," the Ranger reassured him. "I know where the money went. You'll have it all back inside of twenty-four hours, or I'm much mistaken. Mebbe I'm in time to catch the bullion that was taken, too."

As long as he dared, Hatfield remained in Cuevas, waiting for Sheriff Raines. Finally, as the afternoon shadows were growing long, he gave it up and rode swiftly north.

Dusk was falling when he reached the gorge mouth that led to the hidden amphitheater. He did not use the cañon trail, but sent Goldy straight through the hills. He hid the sorrel in a thicket and made the last few hundred yards of the trip on foot. Crouched on the cliff top above the cave, he gazed at the strange scene in the bowl below, clearly outlined in the light of the full moon.

It was no longer empty. Marshaled in the trodden dust were fully five hundred *peónes*. Silently they stood in lines of military precision, evidently awaiting someone. They bore no arms, not even knives in their belts.

Not taking any chances with them till they're shore they've got them under their thumb, he mused, his gaze centering on a tight group of men who stood near a number of horses that showed signs of hard riding.

These men, dark of face, sinister of feature, he knew instantly were the dreaded riders—the inhumanly cruel messengers who were sent forth to summon the *peónes* and to wreak horrible vengeance upon any who refused the summons. They were fully armed with revolvers and knives.

Those are the hombres *I've got to look out for,* Jim Hatfield told himself. *The others down there'll be only too glad to bust loose. All they want to do is tend to their own business and live in peace.*

He lifted his head at the *click* of hoofs drifting up from below. A moment later two men rode into the enclosure. One was short and squat, with a bloated body and stringy black hair. He looked like a giant spider. The other, tall, straight, was muffled to his eyes in a dark serape.

Heads snapped to salute at their entrance. The group of riders, after saluting, turned and moved leisurely toward the mouth of the hidden cave.

Got to get the guns and hand them out, Hatfield instantly deduced. His face was determined and a trifle haggard, as with steady hands cupped to shield the tiny flame he touched a lighted match to the end of the coiled fuse.

I haven't any choice in the matter, the Ranger told himself in self-justification. *Ten of them are too much for me to try to handle by myself. One slip and everything would go to hell. If Raines and the posse were here, it would be different.*

As soon as the fuse was burning, he sped swiftly across the cliff tops and scrambled down to the floor of the cañon. Loosening his guns in their holsters, he strode through the narrow gap and into the dusty bowl. On his breast gleamed the silver star of the Rangers. Suddenly his voice rang out, edged with authority and menace.

"Nobody makes a move!" he shouted. "I've got fifty men with rifles atop those cliffs. You're completely surrounded. One funny trick and there won't be anything but Spanish smoke in hell for the next two days!"

The terrified *peónes* broke ranks and huddled together, staring at the menacing figure that stood, straight and tall, a dozen yards from the bloated spider man and the blanket-swathed figure of his companion.

"Juan Cheno," the Ranger's voice blazed, "you're at the

end of your rope. I've been wanting to catch you on Texas soil for quite a spell. You're under arrest for murder, robbery, and fomenting revolution among American citizens. And that goes for you, too, El Hombre." The Lone Wolf's green eyes blazed at the figure in the serape. "Jerk that blanket off you and show your face, you murdering sidewinder . . . Brant Preston!"

The blanket dropped away, revealing Brant Preston's sinister face, now ghastly in its pallor. In the same instant Cheno, the outlaw, raised his voice in a piercing yell.

"Miguel! Pedro! Felipe!" Terror sounded in his cry. "To me . . . *pronto!*"

From the cave came an answering shout—a shout that was drowned by a crashing roar that shook the very mountains. A mighty flare of reddish light dyed the hill-ringed bowl the color of blood. There was a rumbling of falling rocks and a wild screech of agony and despair.

Flames flickered behind the vines that hid the cave, and there followed volley upon volley of rifle fire. The splintered timbers of the cave were burning, and heat was setting off the thousands of rounds of rifle cartridges.

The *peónes,* remembering the Ranger's threat of rifles ringing the cliff tops, huddled together in a howling, terror-stricken mob. Only Cheno and Preston realized what had really happened and that the threat of rifles was a bluff. With that realization they went for their guns.

Shot for shot, the Lone Wolf answered the blazing revolvers of the pair. Cheno suddenly crumpled and lay still. Hatfield dashed the streaming blood from his eyes and lined sights with Preston's broad breast. His Colt roared again and again.

Preston suddenly ceased firing. Over his face spread a look of vast surprise. The gun dropped from his nerveless fingers, and he sank slowly to the ground. He was dead when the Lone Wolf knelt beside him.

The Ranger had a scalp wound, a nicked shoulder, and a hole through the fleshy part of his left arm. He felt dizzy and a little sick, but he straightened up, wiped the blood from his face, and confronted the awe-struck *peónes*. Fearlessly he walked toward them, his hands empty, nothing but kindness in his green eyes.

"Go to your homes, *amigos,*" he said quietly. "I understand your troubles. I understand why you are here. You don't need to be afraid of El Hombre or The Rider any more. There won't be any revolution. Everything's over with now. Go home to your families."

They crowded around him, laughing, crying, clutching at his hands. Some of the more efficient hastened to bind up his wounds with the skill of much practice.

He was sitting with his back to a rock, smoking a cigarette and feeling much better, when Sheriff Raines at the head of his dust-stained, exhausted posse thundered through the gorge.

Nearly two weeks later, Hatfield sat in Bill McDowell's office and regaled the captain with an account of the happenings in Cuevas County. Sheriff Raines, who had insisted on making the trip with him because of his wound, chuckled as the story progressed.

"Cartina had me puzzled for a while," Hatfield admitted. "Especially that day the stage was robbed. When he came into the saloon that night, he'd said he'd ridden straight from his ranch, and yet his clothes were all covered with dust."

"But, hell," interjected Sheriff Raines, "feller can get dust on his clothes ridin' from his ranch to town."

"Uhn-huh," the Ranger admitted, "he can, but Cartina told me twice that the trail from his place ran over grassland all the way, and, when I asked you how to get there, you told me the same thing. Dust from a trail over grassland is sort of gray-like, or almost white. The dust on Cartina's clothes was reddish . . . the kind of dust you don't get any-where but from those strips of desert that run across the range thereabouts. You'll recollect the stage was robbed on the other side of the desert.

"Cartina was particular to let it be known that he and Kimble had ridden straight from the F Bar C ranch house, and they both had red dust on their clothes. I knew Cartina lied. I knew he'd been on the desert somewhere and wanted to cover it up.

"Of course, what Cartina was trying to do was cover up his ornery half-brother. He didn't know for shore that Kimble was mixed up in the stage robbery, but he sus-pected it, when one of his men brought him the story. He went hunting him . . . that's how come he rode across the desert and got red dust on his clothes. He was making an alibi there in the saloon for Kimble.

"I knew the minute Kimble came in he hadn't ridden to town with Cartina. Cartina had his riders waiting for him out on the trails. They told him what to say. He looked a question to Cartina and waited for his cue before he said anything. Then he played it up.

"Fact is," Hatfield went on, "I first calculated Cartina and Preston were working together. Of course, where Preston made his first slip was in trying to dry-gulch me. It was all too pat . . . Curly Wilkes's leadin' me up that trail to where Preston was holed up. If his rifle hadn't had a busted firing pin and missed fire the second shot, things might've been different. He levered the cartridge out and tried a third one before he realized the trouble was with his rifle. Then he didn't stop to pick up the shells with the splintered firing pin plain on the cap of each one."

"How 'bout the Mexicans in the bunkhouse?" asked Sheriff Raines.

"Preston sent 'em there while riding to Lobo Cañon and the stage robbery," Hatfield said. "He knew the short cut through Pardusco Cañon and knew I would have to take it easy getting back with Wilkes's body. He and Kimble and Kearns and Hilton robbed the stage. Crowley, a new man with the outfit, wasn't in on anything. Preston hired him because he knew he was an escaped convict with a murder charge.

"Preston was half Mexican, but he had served time in Arizona for rustling. Kearns and Hilton and Wilkes were there with him. After they served their time, they got together.

"I'm not just shore which one of 'em first got the idea of the revolution, Preston or his cousin, Cheno. Mebbe Cheno, mebbe Preston, but Preston was educated and Cheno wasn't. Preston led, and Cheno follered. Preston had ambitions, but he knew to tumble Díaz off his perch would take money, lots of it.

"That's where the robbery and rustling came in. They cleaned up close to a quarter of a million dollars altogether. Kimble, being Cartina's half-brother, was in a position to get valuable information about gold shipments and such, and he played it strong. Kimble was on the run from the law and figured, if Preston put his scheme over, he'd be sitting pretty in a country where he'd be safe. Why he killed Hilton nobody will ever know, but there must've been some trouble while we was on the other side of the Río."

"How come Preston was willin' to go into Mexico with

you after Garret?" asked McDowell.

"He calculated it would put him in good with me and with Lonnie's father," Hatfield replied. "He'd figured me for a Ranger and was scared. You see, Kimble recognized me, just as I recognized him. Preston's admitting he knew Kimble in Arizona was what made me write to the warden of the penitentiary there.

"He'd already said he had had some trouble but tried to pass it off as being in Mexico. That was at first, when he was trying to sound me out. Mebbe he'd figured on getting rid of me in Mexico, giving Cheno the word, or something, but I stuck too close to him. He never had a chance to talk to anybody.

"Then, when we got Garret out of jail, Preston got rattled and tried to plug him, making it look like he'd made a mistake because of the whiskers. He knew Garret would tell a different story about the escape than what Preston had told me. When I grabbed his rifle away from him that night, I saw it had a brand-new firing pin.

"I hunted up the gunsmith in Cuevas and found out Preston had had a new firin' pin put in just before we started to Mexico. The old fellow had the busted pin in a junk box, and it tied up with the dent in the cartridge that killed Curly Wilkes. I had him then, but I didn't know where his headquarters were and where he and his riders had their hide-out. I kept hunting through the hills, and, when I pulled that poor fellow out of the snake hole, he told me everything. I found their arsenal and planted dynamite to blow it up.

"I hadn't figured on the riders being in the cave when the dynamite let go, but it all worked out. I'd already found out that Preston was spending money for guns . . . Darnel got that from a Frisco bank he was doing business with . . .

for drafts were made out to big arms dealers.

"The riders, of course, were just Cheno's Yaqui-Mexicans. Preston used 'em to scare hell out of the *peónes,* and they shore did a good job with their torturing and killings. Cutting Ab Carlyle's throat and slicing him up was Kimble's idea to scare hell out of other folks."

He stood up, smiling down at them from his great height.

"Tell *Don* Fernando and Miss Lonnie I'm sorry I can't ride up for the wedding," he remarked to Raines, "but I calculate Cap'n Bill has got another little job waiting for me. I know that look in his eye."

"I shore have," admitted McDowell, "and she's a humdinger, too."

The Lone Wolf looked quite pleased.

"It shore beats hell," said the sheriff, "one Ranger bustin' up a rev'lution single-handed, all by hisself."

"Well," chuckled the Lone Wolf, "you just had one revolution!"

ABOUT THE AUTHOR

LESLIE SCOTT was born in Lewisburg, West Virginia. During the Great War, he joined the French Foreign Legion and spent four years in the trenches. In the 1920s he worked as a mining engineer and bridge builder in the western American states and in China before settling in New York. A barroom discussion in 1934 with Leo Margulies, who was managing editor for Standard Magazines, prompted Scott to try writing fiction. He went on to create two of the most notable series characters in Western pulp magazines. In 1936, when Standard Magazines launched, *Texas Rangers*, Scott, under the house name of Jackson Cole, created Jim Hatfield, Texas Ranger, a character whose popularity was so great with readers that this magazine featuring his adventures lasted until 1958. When others eventually began contributing Jim Hatfield stories, Scott created another Texas Ranger hero, Walt Slade, better known as El Halcón, The Hawk, whose exploits were regularly featured in *Thrilling Western*. In the 1950s Scott moved quickly into writing book-length adventures about both Jim Hatfield and Walt Slade in long series of original paperback Westerns. At the same time, however, Scott was also doing some of his best work in hard cover Westerns published by Arcadia House, thoughtful, well-constructed stories, with engaging characters and authentic settings and situations. Among the best of these are *Silver City* (1953), *Longhorn Empire* (1954), *The Trail Builders* (1956), and *Blood On the Rio Grande* (1959). In these hard cover Westerns, many of which have never been reprinted, Scott proved himself highly capable of writing traditional Western stories with characters who have sufficient depth to change in the course of the narrative and with a degree of authenticity and historical accuracy absent from many of his series stories. *The Texas Ranger* will be his next **Five Star Western**.